MISADVENTURES

WITH

THE BOSS

BY
KENDALL RYAN

MISADVENTURES

WITH

THE BOSS

BY
KENDALL RYAN

WATERHOUSE PRESS

To John.

CHAPTER ONE

PIPER

My Netflix account was judging me.

At least that was how it felt every time I had to insist *Yes, Netflix, I am still watching* Absolutely Fabulous, *thank you very much*. I imagined it asking even more invasive questions— questions my sister would ask if she were here.

Are you sure you want to keep watching?

Didn't you move to New York City for all the exciting nightlife?

And, more importantly—*what kind of twenty-something spends their evening watching so many old sitcoms?*

I grabbed the throw pillow beside me, tucked it under my chin, and snuggled it close to my chest, ignoring the clunk of my phone as it tumbled to the floor. It wasn't like anyone was going to call and ask me to hang out anyway. I was so new to the city that I was still surrounded by boxes that desperately needed to be unpacked.

But not tonight. Tonight, I was determined to sit like a stubborn bump on a lazy log and do nothing.

Raising the remote, I turned up the volume as the theme song faded and the show began. But just as the dialogue was really starting to heat up, my phone broke into the jazzy, happy tone I'd selected for one caller in particular—my sister.

Think of the devil.

I let it play on a bit, debating whether to answer. I then reached for the floor, snagged my phone from the carpet, and pressed it to my face.

"Hello?" I said, waiting for Hailey's chipper voice to fill the speaker.

"Piper," she deadpanned.

"What?" I asked, already feeling defensive and biting back a groan.

First mistake?

Answering the phone.

"Where are you right now? I don't hear anything going on behind you. No music. No chatter. Tell me at least you're at some gallery looking at glorious paintings and sipping champagne," she demanded.

If things were quiet on my end, the same could definitely not be said for hers. As usual, bass-filled music blared behind her voice, getting softer as she moved through whichever Chicago bar was the flavor of the week. There were a lot of things a person could say about Hailey, but nobody could ever accuse her of not knowing her way around a party. To be perfectly honest, I was shocked I didn't hear people chanting her name in the distance, begging her to join them for another shot.

She was like a people magnet, and I was...well, what's the opposite of a people magnet?

Whatever the answer is, that's me.

"I'm home." I stared at the stack of brown cardboard boxes and forced a white lie from my lips because the truth was just too depressing to say. "Unpacking. And can you go outside or something? The music wherever you are is so loud."

"Right." I could practically hear her roll her eyes, but in a matter of minutes, the music had dimmed to practically nothing. "Why aren't you out?"

"Who am I going to go out with?"

"I don't know. You just go out. Find people along the way."

I sighed. "I'm not like you. I don't just enter a room and have people flock to me."

"But aren't you lonely?"

I bit my cheek. "I never said I wasn't."

"So what are you going to do? Just sit around your apartment and hope friends magically appear?"

"I just got a new job. I'll meet people there when I start."

Hailey blew out a frustrated sigh. "This isn't like college or high school. You can't just expect to hang with the people you see all day. We're in the modern age, Pipes. You've gotta throw yourself into it. Take risks. Get wild."

"What, like, join a chat room or something?"

"No, you weirdo. Use an app. All the dating sites have find-a-friend features," she replied matter-of-factly.

"Well, ideally I wouldn't find my friends where people are also trying to get into my pants," I said primly.

"And why not? I'm willing to bet nobody has gotten into your sensible slacks in a good long while, either," my sister said with a snort.

"Hailey," I warned, but she pressed on.

"Come *on*, everybody's doing it," Hailey said. "What could it hurt?"

My pride?

I should have said it aloud, of course, but just like everyone else, I had fallen under the magic spell that Hailey cast on everyone she met. I wanted to please her—to let her have her way. She was just so cool. So everything I wasn't.

"Exactly," Hailey said into the silence. "Even you can't come up with a reason not to. I'm putting you on speaker so I can make you an account right now." There was the sound of fumbling, and then my sister's voice came back over the line again. "Okay, ready. You still have the same email address?"

Sucked into the whirlwind that was Hailey and at a loss to come up with a reason why I shouldn't do this, I nodded, and then catching myself, I said, "Uh, yeah. Same one."

"Great. Now we need to come up with a username for you."

"How about Piper Daniels? My name," I said dryly.

"Do you even internet?" Hailey said with a groan. "No, I think not. We don't need stalkers tracking you down and trying to make dresses out of your skin."

I winced and rubbed at my temple with my fingertip. "If you're trying to convince me this is a good idea, you're not doing a great job."

Frankly, all of this was giving me a tension headache. I glanced longingly at the TV as she continued.

"Relax. We'll root out the weirdos. Now focus. We need a screen name. Think something cute. Something that speaks to who you are as a person."

I paused, but all I could come up with was Piper Longstocking. Between my freckles and my dark-red hair, it was a nickname that had come all too easy to the less-creative relatives in my family. I suggested this to my sister, and as expected, she scoffed.

"Jesus. God, no. Nothing about that screams sexy to me."

"I'm not trying to scream sexy. I'm trying to find friends," I reminded her.

"Well, we're keeping our options open," she hedged in a way that made the hairs on the back of my neck stand up. "Besides, there's going to be a picture of you on the profile. I used that one from cousin Anna's wedding."

"The one where I'm sneezing?" I hissed, mortified.

"No. What do you take me for, woman? There's another one. You look cute, trust me. Now, let's focus this name on something you like to do or something about you. You're all organized, right? What about something to do with that?"

"Planning Piper?" I suggested.

"I don't like it. We need to make it sexier."

"Hail—"

"I've got it. Okay. Typed and saved. Can't change it now."

"I'm afraid to ask," I groaned.

"Oh, it's nothing bad. Just, you know, roll with the punches."

"And what punches am I rolling with?"

She mumbled at first, so low that I couldn't hear her.

"What was that?" I asked.

"Fantasy Girl 29," she said more clearly.

"What?" I yelped. "Are you serious? What kind of person

is looking to be friends with someone who names herself Fantasy Girl 29?"

"What? You love fantasy stuff. You're all into, like, *Game of Thrones* and *Lord of the Rings,* so I thought—"

"That is not how people are going to read that, Hail."

"Oh well. What's done is done," she said in a rush. "Now we just need to answer some questions. You're a 29-year-old female with a bangin' bod, and you're looking for friendship, long- and short-term relationships, and casual sex."

Panic shot through me, and I let out a squeak. "I am not looking for—"

"Aren't you?" Hailey cut in. "Be honest with me for just a second here. What would it really hurt for you to get a good, rough bone in every now and again? It's been ages since you and Tommy broke up, and I seriously doubt you found yourself a fuck boy to get over it, so—"

I wrinkled my nose. "No, I moved to a new city to start fresh and get away from him. Now come on, don't—"

"Too late. Already done," Hailey chirped. "No going back now."

I pinched my nose between two fingers. "Right. Of course not."

"Now let's answer some questions. You drink occasionally, and you don't smoke. Those are easy. You're an animal person."

"I'm allergic to cats," I said.

"But you like them. Good enough."

"Why do I get the feeling I should hang up and just let you do whatever you're going to do?"

"Come on, don't be like that," she pleaded in that sweet

voice that made me want to hand her the moon on a platter. "Now let's get to the real questions, shall we? Okay, if you were going to have one romantic night anywhere in the world, where would you choose?"

I thought hard. Some girls would say Paris. Others would say a picnic on the edge of a lake.

Me? I glanced at my paused TV and said, "In my apartment. Homemade dinner and some movies. Perfect night."

Hailey groaned. "I'll never understand how we came from the same people's loins, but I'm writing it down because I love you, and surely there is someone out there who will too. Okay, next one. On a scale of one to ten, how adventurous are you?"

"One," I said.

"Five, then," Hailey corrected. "Nobody says one. They'll think you cower in your apartment like a hermit, afraid to leave the house."

"That's kind of what I do."

"But people don't need to know that."

And so it went. Over and over again—for roughly a million questions—Hailey asked me about myself and then corrected me to make me more palatable to other people. When at last we'd finished, she clicked into my profile and let out a contented sigh.

"Okay, here's your description. Hey there! I'm Piper, and I'm looking for like-minded people to hang out with as I'm new to the city. My interests include Netflix, a good glass of wine, board games, and snuggly couches," Hailey said.

"Good enough," I said, compromising because it was the

best I was going to get from her at this point.

"Great," she said, smacking her lips with satisfaction. "Ooh, lookie here! You've already got a match."

"What?" My stomach kicked up a team of butterflies. "Are you serious?"

"Dead. Oh, wow," Hailey cooed. "He's sexy."

"I'm not looking for sexy," I reminded her.

"Oh, you're *definitely* looking for this kind of sexy. Everyone wants this kind of sexy. Holy cow."

"How do you know he's not going to make a wig out of my skin or whatever you said?" I reminded her, trying not to let the panic set in.

"Oh, relax. You can keep me on speed dial through your whole date."

"Date?" I asked.

"It's tomorrow night at the Florentine Inn. That place is nice, so wear a dress," she chirped.

"What the hell, Hail?" I said, my palms going clammy even at the thought.

"Don't worry, you don't have to thank me just yet."

"Cancel it," I shot back. "Cancel it right now."

"No. You need to get out there, and this is the only way you're ever going to do it. I'm just giving you a gentle shove, sis," Hailey insisted.

It felt more like a knife in my back. Everything in me wanted to fight her on this. Everything except this one, teeny tiny part of me that feared she was right—and I was terrified to spend the rest of my life alone. Of sitting inside this apartment with no one to talk to and nothing to do and, worse, getting more comfortable with it day by day until the only people I saw were workmates and Thai food delivery guys. That part had me considering it. Just this one time.

"Well, tell me something about him, at least," I grumbled.

"Nope. You have to go into this with an open mind, and at least this way, I know you will."

For a female, the size of my sister's balls never failed to astonish me. "You're evil," I said.

"Yep, but you are going to like this guy and end up thanking me. I can feel it. Now I've gotta go. When I left, some chick was talking about riding the mechanical bull, and I'm pretty sure it's about to get hilarious in there. Love you."

She hung up, and I glared at my phone for a long moment before setting it on the coffee table in front of me and staring at the TV.

I couldn't remember the last time I'd been on a first date—maybe not since college. I'd thought, way back when, that Tommy and I were going to make it, that we'd get married. But no. He got promoted to Head Douchebag or whatever his title was at some real estate firm, and he left me in the dust. And then, with his face plastered on every billboard in town promoting the firm, I couldn't get away from the guy.

I'd needed a fresh start—something new. Different. So I came here.

And I've been wallowing and watching Netflix ever since. Though, to be fair, it had only been three days.

Placing my hands just outside my thighs, I propelled myself from the couch and made my way toward the calendar hanging from my fridge. Monday was marked with bright-green ink—my first day at my new job. And tomorrow?

Tomorrow was a day for pink. The color of romance.

I picked a pen from a little cup near the fridge, wrote the time and place of my date on the calendar, and then stood back and smiled. Hailey could be right. This could be my one chance to get back on the horse and spend my Friday nights somewhere other than lounging on my couch alone.

And she was right about one other thing too.

It had been a long, long time since I'd felt the warmth of a man's skin against me. And the fact that I didn't know a thing about this guy? Well, that made it all the more terrifying...but also kind of exciting.

The best part? If it didn't work out, I'd never have to see him again. Maybe Hailey had really come up with the perfect plan this time.

CHAPTER TWO

JACKSON

The tension was starting to get to me.

Which, I should note, was extremely rare. Mergers fell through and clients backed out, but me? I was cool as a fucking cucumber straight out of the refrigerator.

Except, of course, in times like these...

When I'd gone more than two weeks without getting laid.

It was like clockwork, really. The moment the clock stroked two weeks, I was like a caged animal, tense and pacing, waiting for some brief moment of release. And now, two hours after I should have gone home for the day and one hour after my assistant should have ordered my dinner? I was more pent-up than ever before.

Hungry and horny was almost too much to bear. Horngry. It was a bad combination all around.

Stalking toward my desk, I pressed down on the intercom and said, "Jane, I need you to find me a date for tomorrow night. Some internet site or something should be fine. And when is dinner supposed to get here?"

I released the button and waited for Jane's nervous, skittering voice to buzz through the line. Nothing happened.

I held back a growl and paced to the door, opening it to find... nothing.

An empty desk with a neat lavender note folded in half and labeled with my name.

Taking it, I unfolded the letter and skimmed its contents.

Mr. Dane,

By the time you read this, I'm sure I'll have been gone for hours. I'm sorry to leave this way, but I simply can't work like this anymore. I need to have a job where I can be sure I'll be able to pick up my children on time and make them supper. As I stated in my initial interview, this isn't something I'm willing to compromise.

I informed HR of my departure two weeks ago—a fact I'm sure they told you but you've allowed to slip your mind. Thank you for the opportunity, and I'm sorry it didn't work out. As I'm sure I'll not be receiving a recommendation from you anyway, and this job will not be listed on my résumé, please allow me to provide you with some advice for dealing with future assistants.

I can't read your mind. Nobody can read your mind. And you can't work people like they were born specifically to serve you.

Good luck finding someone who will be able to meet your insane standards.

Regards,

Jane Clarence

I blinked, reading over the last paragraph again. She had

a hell of a lot of nerve telling me what I could and couldn't do when she barely knew how to type, file, or keep a damn schedule.

Tossing the letter into the recycling bin, I made a mental note to confront HR first thing on Monday about my lack of assistant. I'd go straight to the head of the department—after all, there was no reason I should have had to train eight assistants in the past three months unless the candidates they were providing me were subpar.

Clearly, there was a systemic issue at play here that needed to be addressed.

With a muttered groan, I settled into the chair behind my desk. I pulled up the Meals-to-Go app on my phone and ordered in some dinner and then opened a browser for a list of dating sites.

I hated this. Hated every last detail of having to enter my personality type and what I was looking for in a soul mate. Because, you know what? I wasn't looking for a soul mate. I wasn't even looking for a girlfriend. I was looking for a quick, casual piece of ass. A good time in exchange for a guaranteed good time.

I briefly considered just heading to the nearest nightclub and hoping for the best. Fact was, it usually worked out in the end, but the last thing I wanted to do after a long week at work was spend four hours in a noisy club in exchange for an hour or two in the sheets. Especially if it meant having to extricate myself from a needy woman who had missed the memo. I shuddered at the thought.

I'm not an asshole. I don't lie or make promises I can't

keep. But some women just can't shake the feeling that every guy they sleep with might be "the one."

PSA: I'm not "the one." And I will never be "the one."

Which was why I opted to click on a site notorious for no-strings hookups.

I downloaded the app and entered all the usual information before searching the database of women looking for casual sex, just like me.

With a bunch of them, I could tell it was a ploy at first glance. There was a needy hope in their gazes. Like, they'd say all the right things, but deep down they hoped that as soon as some poor sucker saw what was underneath their dress, they'd magically want something more from them than a good lay.

Those girls, of course, I avoided like the plague.

And the girls who said their idea of a romantic night was a candlelit dinner in Paris?

No thanks.

I didn't need a night with a dreamer. I wanted a dirty, uncomplicated romp.

Which was when the sixth girl in my matches caught my eye and made my cock pulse.

She wasn't my usual supermodel-lean type of girl. Her cheeks were full and smooth, rounding out a perfect, heart-shaped face, and her long mane of dark-red hair looked soft as silk—but it was something in her broad smile that made me click on the picture and read on.

In the description, there was another picture of her. In this one, she was dancing on a table, her wild hair flying behind her while she kicked out her feet and laughed at the camera.

She wore a low-cut black dress that accentuated her luscious curves. I swallowed hard before glancing at her bio.

She liked Netflix and comfy couches. She was an animal person and a busy professional. All her sentences were quick and to the point—she wasn't trying to impress anyone. Which meant maybe, just maybe, she meant what she said. I double-checked she had indeed checked off that she was interested in casual sex, and then I bit the bullet and sent her a message.

Jackson21782: *Hey, you interested in dinner and hooking up tomorrow?*

Quick and to the point. If she wasn't interested, I'd move on to the next girl. No harm, no foul.

Within a matter of seconds, though, my screen dinged, and I clicked over to see a response.

Fantasy Girl 29: *Absolutely. Name the time and place.*

Jackson 21782: *Florentine Inn. 6 o'clock.*

I paused, and figured, fuck it. Might as well make sure she knew the score right out the gate.

Jackson 21782: *Don't wear underwear.*

I waited, mildly curious to see what her reply would be. A second later, my screen dinged again.

Fantasy Girl 29: *I can't make any promises.*

I grinned at that and scrolled back to her image, feeling

satisfied and already a little less tense just thinking of our date. One slow, hard fuck, and I'd be right as rain. Then, when I came in on Monday, I'd be able to deal with this whole HR problem without wanting to rip people's heads off at every turn.

I closed the app's messenger and penned the meeting into my date book, secretly wondering if she might dance on the table for me without her panties on tomorrow night if I asked nicely.

Damn, would that be one hell of a view...

♦ ♦ ♦ ♦

During my work day on Friday, I pushed the date from my mind, focusing instead on the upcoming merger and the innumerable speeches I'd be forced to make at any given press junket or business conference. Of course, the fact that I had no assistant made that task all the more difficult. After a few fumbling tries with the new management software, I was quickly getting the hang of things. I'd set up a meeting with Sally from HR but had been forced to cancel when a new real estate listing had fallen through the cracks and required my attention. I was so busy, the rest of my day went by in a blur.

In fact, I barely even thought about Fantasy Girl 29.

The end of the day came just as quickly as the start, and before I knew it, five o'clock had finally come around. As usual, I was going to stay behind for a while to work—the restaurant for our meetup was just around the corner—but before I settled into the pile of listings I'd set aside to go through, I picked up the receiver and dialed Human Resources.

Sally, the head of the department, answered the phone in

monotone. "Jackson."

"Sally, how did you know it was me?"

"Who else would be calling me at five o'clock on a Friday?" she asked. "Everyone else is gone. Can we make this quick, Jackson? I have dinner plans with my husband."

I resisted the urge to play the world's tiniest violin for her, but she had a strong work ethic and typically got the job done, which tipped the scale in her favor in my book.

Except with this whole assistant thing. That was out of hand.

"When will the agency be sending over a new candidate for me to interview?" I asked, jumping right to the point.

"Oh no, you're not interviewing them anymore. In fact, the agency stopped working with us when the last two candidates left here in tears. I hired this one myself."

"What? Why?" I demanded.

"Something to do with unrealistic expectations, boss. You're burning through their candidates faster than they can send them."

"Ridiculous. I think maybe we ought to get a new system for vetting candidates so I can—"

"No, I don't think so. In fact, our legal team has advised me that your behavior could be stepping into hostile work environment territory, and they've asked me to handle the details of your staff from here on out. Your new assistant starts on Monday. If she doesn't work out, you can talk to our counsel and tell them you want to hire the next one yourself."

"And when am I supposed to find time for that? You know we're on the verge of a possible merger with Global Business

Solutions." I didn't mean to snap, but the words definitely came out a little clipped.

"Which is exactly why legal wants to keep us out of lawsuit territory. At this rate, I think the only person who'll work for you is a superhero. Nobody can keep your insane hours. I know this place is your baby, and you're amazing at the business side of things, but my advice? Honestly, sir. You need to back off."

I wanted to reprimand her, but frankly, half the reason I'd hired her was for the straight talk. Yes-people were part of the game, but maybe-not-sir-people were twice as valuable.

"Right, well, thanks for the help, Sally," I said finally with a frustrated sigh.

"Yup. Have a good weekend."

The line died, and I put the receiver back down and stared at it for a long moment.

I wasn't impossible to work for. I was exacting, yes, but I never asked for anything I couldn't do myself. That was important when it came to being a boss. Or, at least, that's what I used to think.

Again, the tension inside me rose, and I considered phoning my hookup and asking her to come straight to my office in nothing but a trench coat and some thigh-high boots. Unfortunately for me, that was what strippers and prostitutes did—not random strangers from a damn internet app. The least I could do was buy the woman a nice meal and a good bottle of Cabernet.

For a second, I allowed myself to fantasize about something easy. A long-term casual arrangement with a woman—someone who knew what I needed and when and didn't have to get her heart involved. Someone who didn't want a ring or children but just raw, carnal satisfaction.

That was all I was good for, and that was exactly what I wanted in return.

"Just be happy you're at least getting laid tonight," I muttered to myself.

Tapping my fingers against the arms of my chair, I considered the files piled high on my desk and shrugged. Tomorrow was a new day, and I could always stop by and pick up the files to work on them from home over the weekend. I needed out of here, stat.

I grabbed my jacket and made for the elevators on the far side of my floor. I would be early for my date, but I needed a good stiff drink, and I couldn't sit around here waiting any longer—I felt like a damned caged animal.

Shoving my hands into the pockets of my jacket, I headed toward the Florentine Inn around the corner and sidled up to the bar, ignoring the interested glances of the waitresses I passed.

"Sapphire martini, dry as a bone, three olives," I told the bartender, and he offered me a little nod before setting to work. As I waited, I stared at the door, willing the girl I'd seen online to stroll in, laughing like she had in her pictures.

Fuck dinner.

When I saw her, I was going to corner her and suggest we have a drink or two and then get straight to the main event. Even now, I could feel my blood running hotter at the thought of sinking deep into her hot, tight—

"Your drink, sir."

The bartender set my glass in front of me, and I took a sip and tried to relax. I enjoyed my drink and the quiet of my thoughts for a few minutes before my gaze ventured to the door again and landed on a woman who was unmistakably the one I'd been looking for. She was walking through the wide glass doors with pink cheeks and wind-swept hair. A long tan trench coat hugged those supple curves, but based on the hint of cleavage peaking out from under her coat, I knew the pictures hadn't been a lie.

She was stacked, a perfect hourglass my hands itched to trace.

Still, as she walked toward the bar on long, shapely legs, I couldn't help but think she didn't look like the one-night-stand type. She looked...sweet. Almost innocent. Maybe it was something to do with her wide blue eyes or the curve of her full, luscious lips. More school girl than call girl.

When she smiled at me, though, all my blood rushed south, and I realized that nice in the streets and naughty in the sheets was okay by me.

She had a mouth and a body built for pleasure, and I couldn't wait to make her scream.

Fantasy Girl 29 indeed.

CHAPTER THREE

PIPER

I felt naked.

Not just in that fresh-out-of-the-shower way, either. Nope. As his penetrating gaze raked over me, I felt raw and exposed, like someone had pulled my skirt down in a crowd of people and I couldn't do anything to fix it. The weirdest part was, I didn't hate it.

Heat was rushing to my cheeks, and for a moment, I considered tucking tail and running from the bar, but something inside me kept me moving and making my way toward the man who hadn't stopped staring at me since I'd walked in. Maybe it was the fact that, for the first time since I got to New York, I felt energized. Excited. Full of anticipation.

There was no doubt in my mind this was the guy I was going for. After all, he was exactly Hailey's type. His dark hair was a little shaggy but well kept, and his dark eyes were soulful and hot, assessing me and, based on the slight smile on his chiseled lips, liking what he saw.

Which only made my blush deepen.

He was too handsome and intimidating to be the kind of guy I normally would have gone for. Based on his perfectly tailored dark-blue suit, I had to guess he'd come straight from work, but even now, in the bar, he hadn't bothered to loosen his tie or take off his jacket.

No, he looked like he was ready to make a fresh acquisition.

And based on the hungry look in his eye? I knew exactly what kind of merger he had in mind.

You can do this.

Clearing my throat as I reached him, I forced a friendly smile and stuck out my hand.

"Hi there. I'm Piper."

"Nice to meet you." His warm palm swallowed my hand, and he gave me one confident pump before releasing me and motioning to the chair beside him. "Jackson. What's your drink?"

"Pear vodka and cranberry," I said automatically.

"Interesting combo," he said with a half smile.

"When you taste it, it makes perfect sense. Sweet and tart and delicious. Heaven in a glass." I slid onto the little stool, and Jackson summoned the bartender with a wave of his hand. When the other man approached, he ordered my drink and then watched as the bartender set to work.

Following his lead, I watched too and was overcome with a swell of gratitude when I saw exactly how much vodka the guy poured for me. Something about tonight made me feel like I was going to need every last drop.

"So, I, uh, feel like I should tell you that I don't usually do this." I glanced at him from the corner of my eye and tucked an errant strand of hair behind my ear.

"It's easy," Jackson said. "You'll get the hang of it."

I nodded. "I guess just being in a new city always has its learning curves."

"I'm sure."

"Have you ever moved someplace new without knowing anybody?" I asked.

He considered me for a long moment and then shook his head. "I travel a lot, but I've always lived in the city."

"I see. So...you travel."

He took a sip of his drink, surveying me over the rim. God, what I wouldn't do to get him to stop looking at me like that. Like I was the next, most delicious course on the menu. It made me hot in all the right places, but it also made it hard to focus on anything he was saying.

"I do," he said simply.

"For work? What sort of job do you have?"

He shook his head. "For work, yeah, but I don't want to talk about work. I want to talk about you."

"Me?" I raised my eyebrows and then gave the bartender a grateful nod as he set my drink in front of me.

"You. There's nobody else in the room more interesting." He offered me another smile, and I glanced away, my heart beating harder in my chest.

"I don't know about that." I took a swig of my drink.

"You don't have to. I already know. Now tell me about yourself."

I let out a nervous laugh. "Not much to tell. My sister actually set up my profile."

"Really?"

I nodded. "Younger. You know how they can be."

"I don't. Only child." He shrugged.

"Oh, well, you'd think that the older sibling is the one who thinks they know everything, but when it comes to Hailey—my sister—it's totally different. My parents let her get away with murder, so she basically thinks a person can do anything they want."

"And why can't they?" He raised his eyebrows.

"Well..." I swallowed hard. "You know, responsibilities and stuff."

"So what do you want to do right now that you feel like you can't? What would your sister do?"

Rip your clothes off and tell you to have your way with me...

No, wait. Where did that even come from?

I swallowed hard and shook my head. "Nothing comes to mind."

"Well, you tell me when something does."

I nodded, sucking in my cheeks as I looked away for what felt like the millionth time. The intensity of his gaze was beginning to get to me, and already I wanted to fan myself, despite the comfortable temperature of the room.

"Tell me something else," he said, and his fingers brushed against mine.

I glanced down, all too aware of the electric tingle coursing through my body at his touch.

"I don't know," I spluttered. "But I'm starting to wonder what my sister wrote about me on my profile."

"You haven't seen it?" He raised his eyebrows.

"Nope. Like I said, she does what she wants."

"But you're still here. Why?" he asked, cocking his head

and eyeing me speculatively.

"Because...I was curious," I admitted.

"And is your curiosity satisfied now?" He sipped his drink.

I opened my mouth to answer and then closed it. Why did it feel like everything out of this guy's mouth was just some method to get me to admit that I wanted him, rough and ready, from the second I'd laid eyes on him?

And, more importantly, why did I like that about him?

What was happening to me? Where was homebody, keep-to-herself Piper?

"You're not the usual kind of guy I see," I confessed, hoping he wouldn't notice my sudden change of subject.

"No?" he asked. "How is that?"

"You're just different."

"I got that." The slight smile returned, and I took another sip of my drink to steady myself.

"Do you always dress like this?" I pointed to his suit.

"Duty calls. I work a lot."

"Yeah, I was getting that vibe," I said.

"And what other vibe are you getting?"

That you want me to slide off my panties and give them to you as a trophy?

"That you're used to getting what you want," I said, compromising. That was true too and a little safer.

"I am." This time the smile was a full-on grin, like a wolf who'd just spotted a tasty-looking sheep.

My heart thudded a little faster in my chest, and I gripped my drink, swirling it nervously.

It was safe to say this was the most intense—and somehow

terrifying—conversation I'd ever had with a man, but I still couldn't work up the courage to get up and go.

And more than that?

I didn't want to. Not even a little bit. My blood was singing as my brain tried to imagine what would happen from here.

Something about this guy—whether it was his dark stare or the way he smiled like he hadn't had much practice at it— intrigued me. Attracted me. Just looking at his rugged square jaw made me need to squeeze my thighs together to quell the ache rising there.

He was the most handsome man I'd ever set eyes on, and there was no doubt what he wanted from me...and what I wanted to give him in return.

Swallowing hard, I forced myself to press on, if only to avoid being swallowed up by his gaze.

"Actually, uh"—I cleared my throat—"I didn't see your profile. My sister just sort of picked you for me."

"And you're starting to wonder what it says about me? Since I'm so different than the guys you normally hook up with and all?" He raised his eyebrows, his lips tilting into a slight smirk.

"Sort of." If he only knew.

"I can tell you in a nutshell." He took a sip of his drink. "The picture of me is from a magazine article I was in a few years back."

"Magazine?"

He nodded. "I don't actually like the picture, but it was handy."

"Apparently it was enough to impress my sister," I said.

"And is she less discerning than you? Is that why I'm so different from your usual dates?"

I smiled, starting to relax into our banter for a brief second. "That's not what I said."

"But is it what you meant?"

I glanced away and swirled my drink, thinking hard. "I'm just...a low-key kind of girl. I'm betting that magazine was, what...forty under forty successful bachelors?"

"Close. Thirty under thirty. It was a few years ago." He tipped his glass toward me in silent cheers for the guess.

"See? Yeah, I've never been out with a guy like you."

"Until now."

"Until now," I agreed.

"And what do you think so far?" he asked, his gaze appraising me.

That I'm in way over my head...

That you're out of my league...

"That..." I weighed a few more answers but couldn't escape the truth. "That I have no idea what I'm doing with someone like you."

"Do you want to know a secret?" he asked, momentarily catching me off guard.

"Sure."

"I'm just like every other man you've ever met. When I look at you, I see a beautiful woman who I'd very much like to take back to my place and undress, one piece of clothing at a time."

"That wouldn't be very hard since I'm only wearing a dress." I let out a nervous laugh and ignored the urge to slap my forehead and curse my own stupidity.

"Don't think that hasn't occurred to me." His voice was low and husky, and followed by a predator's grin.

I swallowed hard. "I'm betting you're not the kind of guy who wants to chat over breakfast tomorrow morning."

"You'd be a winner if you made that bet. I think you like that about me." He snubbed a hand over his jaw and then moved closer, tucking an errant strand of hair behind my ear as he leaned in closer.

"I can tell you what I want from you down to the very last detail, but it can't be here," he whispered, his warm breath sending an involuntary shudder through me.

"Why not?" I breathed, captivated.

My heart thrummed in my chest, in my ears, in my lips, and I closed my eyes, savoring the sweet smell of his aftershave as he inched still closer to me—so close that I could feel the heat radiating from his body.

"Because when I tell you what I need from you, we're going to be in private. And I'm guessing you'll give me everything I ask for."

It wasn't a question. It was a demand. There would be no courtship here. No shy undressing and awkward first time. No giggling as he fumbled with the hook of my bra and pressed chaste kisses along the column of my throat.

Whatever happened between us, it was going to be rough and needy and passionate. But more than that, it was going to be exactly the way he wanted it.

And my curiosity about what that entailed was getting the better of me.

"So where do you suggest we go, then?" I asked.

He smiled wide, flashing a dimple I hadn't yet seen. "I have just the place."

I took one last sip of my drink, knowing I'd need a little liquid courage, and offered him my hand.

Jackson set some money on the bar and whisked me out onto the street.

CHAPTER FOUR

JACKSON

The property was just around the corner, so we didn't have far to walk. It was also on the edge of the industrial part of the city, and it looked every bit the remnant of a time long past. The walls were a dusty gray, and the steel framework surrounding the factory-like architecture was less than inviting.

For a moment, her sure grip slackened in my hand, and I squeezed her palm, reassuring her.

"We're here," I said.

"Which is where?" she asked hesitantly.

"It was a lightbulb factory," I said as I motioned to the dark exterior. "Can't really tell that now."

"And you brought me here because...?" She raised her eyebrows.

"Because I have something I want to show you. You've just got to trust me." I pulled out my phone and entered the code for the Bluetooth lock, opening the creaky, rusted gate, and then motioned for her to join me.

"Look, as much as I love following strangers from the internet into abandoned warehouses, I'm going to have to take a hard pass here."

I grinned, not for the first time tonight, and handed her my phone. Sexy and funny. It was a heady combination and one I hadn't seen in a very long time.

"Here. You can hold on to this if it makes you feel better. You can even get 9-1-1 cued up and ready to go. And, by the way, there's a GPS tracker for blind dates on the dating app we used to meet, you know."

Some of the apprehension cleared from her pretty face, and her expressive sapphire eyes filled with relief. "Clever."

She held on to the phone, though, as she followed me into the massive hallway, our footsteps echoing off the walls as we made our way to the elevator.

"How do you know about this place?" she asked.

"My company owns it. We just bought it, actually. I was here a few days ago, but nobody in town will see us. They all think the place is haunted."

"I can't see why," she said with an eye roll.

She followed me into the lift and waited as it groaned to life. After a long pause, we began our slow ascent. I looked at her from the corner of my eye.

She really was gorgeous. In fact, she was likely the hottest woman I'd been out with in ages but totally different at the same time. She didn't have the same cool, almost chilly exterior I was used to, and despite her even features, wide eyes, full lips, and ridiculous curves, she seemed wholly unaware of the package she created. She was comfortable in her skin, I could tell that much, but she wasn't cocky about her looks either. I was guessing she wasn't at all interested in Botoxing and manicuring herself to the last degree. Somehow I liked that.

The elevator stalled and then yawned open, the grated doors sliding apart. Above us, the warm spring day was cooling into night and the clear, blue sky was fading into violet and maroon.

"You brought me to the roof," she said, but then she turned around to face me. "How does a place like this have this kind of roof?"

I offered her half a smile. I'd known that it would impress her. If it hadn't, I never would have brought her here to begin with.

Since when did you feel the need to impress a one-night stand? a little voice piped in. But I quieted it with a mental smackdown. All that mattered was that we had all the makings of a hot night in front of us.

The cement tile of the roof had been converted into an urban garden, complete with flower beds and a twinkle-lit grotto with cushy casual seating and a fire pit. Vines climbed up every wall, and the curved opening to the grotto invited us with a soft gust of wind.

Walking toward it, I pressed a button to light the fireplace and then flicked on the sea of miniature lights, watching as Piper's eyes widened in surprise.

"We're converting the factory into high-end apartments. This will be a community area. We wanted the whole place to be green and organic to fit a certain type of buyer. The interior designer needed to do it first so the plants had time to grow and flourish here. What do you think?"

"I think...this place is incredible." She settled onto the plush red sofa beneath the concave glass ceiling of the grotto, the twinkling lights shining in her eyes.

"The soft light suits you. It brings out the color in your eyes," I said.

Her smile faltered for a moment as my gaze met hers, and that familiar, curious glow overtook her cheeks.

"What's on your mind?" I asked.

She blushed a deeper crimson. "Nothing."

I took a seat beside her, leaned close, and cupped her chin, forcing her to meet my gaze. "Come on, tell me."

Her eyes blazed with something unreadable, and then she wet her lips. "Well, we're in private now. So I was thinking of what you said before...about how you were going to tell me what you want."

Her words hit me straight below the belt, and my cock went instantly stiff. Brushing a loose strand of hair behind her ear, I moved closer still, my warm breath against the shell of her ear. "First, I want to kiss you."

And then I did. Just a brush of lips over those full trembling lips of hers. She shivered at my touch, and I cupped the nape of her neck, holding her closer to me. "Then I want to watch you undress for me."

"But..." Her voice was nothing more than a whisper.

"No buts," I murmured. "I want to see you. All of you."

Again there was another flicker of hesitation, so long this time that I wondered if she might duck out altogether. Instead, though, she slid away from me and stood just beside the fire, the light flickering on her creamy skin.

Slowly, carefully, she reached behind her and unfastened the buttons of her dress. Then, gripping the hem of the fabric, she pulled it over her head and allowed her hair to brush down against her naked collarbone.

Beneath the dress, she wore nothing but sheer white panties and a matching bra that highlighted the long, smooth plane of her stomach and the curve of her full breasts. She shifted slightly as I drank in her toned, shapely legs. My throat was dry as fuck now, but I managed to grit out another command.

"Everything," I muttered, pointing to the scrap of lace covering her. "Off. I want to see you."

"And what about you?" she asked, though it didn't stop her from unfastening the clasp of her bra.

"In time. But I've been imagining what you look like under that dress all night."

She let the bra fall to the floor, and my gaze raked over her tight, pink nipples. They were straining peaks waiting for me to suck and tease, and if it hadn't been for the fact that she was already reaching for her panties, I might have closed the distance between us and forgotten my earlier demands.

As it was, though, she stepped from her underwear and showed me the trimmed patch of hair leading to the spot I wanted to lap with my tongue and tease until my name on her lips was the only sound filling the night air.

Blood rushed to my ears as I held back a groan, suddenly feeling every single second of the past couple of celibate weeks in full force.

"Now get on that sofa, spread your legs, and touch

yourself."

"But you—" she started.

"I'm used to getting what I want," I finished for her.

She closed her mouth and followed my command, her fingers drifting gently to her folds and teasing the space there in rhythmic little circles.

Goddamn, that was sexy. Watching her, I loosened my tie and slid it off, and then started on the buttons of my shirt.

As I went, I watched her, and her gaze never left mine.

"You want to know what I want?" I said. "I want to watch you play with yourself until you're nice and wet for me. Then, when you're so ready for me you want to scream, I'm going to get on my knees in front of you and lick that pretty pink space between your legs until you come with my name on your lips."

Her breath hitched, and I tossed aside my shirt, making way for my pants.

"Then, when you've come so hard you're not sure you can ever come again, I'm going to show you what it's really like to have a man inside you. I'm going to make you claw my back and beg for release."

"And then what?" Her voice was needy, breathy, and she moved her hand faster with every word, delicate little strokes that made my blood hot and my hands quake with the need to touch her.

"Then maybe I'll let you come while I'm inside you. Maybe." I stepped from my pants and pulled off my socks. Then, in nothing but my boxers, I took another step toward her. "Now tell me, do you want me to kiss you, Piper?"

She gave me a quick, needy nod, and I sank to my knees

in front of her, kissing my way up her thigh until I found the place where her fingers still lingered. Then, taking each finger in turn, I kissed the tips and pushed them aside to see her slick pink clit.

"Fuck," I growled, feeling almost light-headed with the weight of my need for her.

"I'm close," she warned with a stunned little laugh. "Like, so close."

"I know," I said, and then I circled the tight bundle of nerves with the tip of my tongue before dipping lower, laving her slick folds and teasing her sweet pink center. Delicious. Hot silk drenched in honey. All rational thought collapsed as I delved deeper, stroking now, faster...harder.

"Jackson," she hummed, her fingers driving into my hair, anchoring me closer.

"Yeah, that's it," I murmured against her, the scent of her driving me wild, making my heart pump double-time. "Say it. Say my name."

She obliged, the hum turning into a low chant as I worked her plump, swollen flesh. She trembled, and I gripped her hip with one hand as I slid the other between her satin thighs. Higher and higher until I felt it. That wet, needy heat.

She held her breath, freezing below me as I pushed a finger inside her tight channel.

My cock gave a needy throb as her tight grip closed around my finger, hugging me in a carnal embrace.

"Ah, Jackson!"

I could feel it in her every move, hear it in her voice. She was going to come, and I couldn't fucking wait for it.

I nudged that tight bundle of nerves again in the lightest of caresses and felt her walls break apart at my touch. She shuddered, writhing into my mouth with quick, frenzied jerks of her hips. Her fingers weaved tighter through my hair, burying my face against her, willing me to consume her...work her through until the very last tremor subsided.

And I did. All the while, I listened as she called my name like a prayer, twitching and flexing, milking every last drop of pleasure from her climax. When it was finally over, she fell back onto her elbows, gasping.

"That was...wow." She shook her head, face glowing as she smiled down at me. "That has never happened so fast."

I heard her words, but they were far away, obliterated by the blood that still pounded in my ears like a heartbeat. I wasn't done. Not even close.

"We're just getting started," I ground out, pressing one last long, sucking kiss to that sweet, soft flesh before pulling away and withdrawing my finger with not a little regret. She was hot. Like fire. So responsive and sensual, but I could already feel the droplets of come weeping from the slit of my manhood, and my balls were aching. She'd come again. I'd make sure of it. But she was going to come wrapped around my shaft so I could feel it.

I got back to my feet, paced to my slacks, and grabbed the condom I kept there for just these sorts of occasions. Ripping the foil carefully, I stepped out of my boxers and then slid the latex over my aching length.

I gripped myself, hoping to quell the now-painful need surging inside me, but when her gaze fell on my member, her eyes widened and she gave me yet another slight shake of the head.

"Jackson, I..."

This wasn't the first time I'd seen that expression. She was nervous, and seeing exactly how hard I was, I couldn't blame her. She was a tight little thing, and I had been blessed in the size department. What could I say?

"Tell me you don't want me," I murmured, stroking up and down, a bolt of satisfaction rushing through me as her gaze followed my motions and she wet her lips.

"It's not that." Her words were soft, and I knew she meant every last one of them.

"Good," I said, "because it's time for round two."

After that, there were no words of protest. Instead, she wriggled closer to the edge of the sofa and parted her legs, making way for me to join her.

"No," I said, sitting down in the space she'd just left. I took her hand and guided her closer. She dropped it to my hard length and stroked me with her tantalizingly soft palm. It was almost enough to make me forget what I'd wanted. Her sweet, tentative stroke on my needy, rock-hard flesh. But then I pictured her above me, gorgeous tits bouncing, mouth parted as she cried out, and I shook my head again.

"You're going to ride me, baby. Fast or slow. It's up to you. I just want to feel you come around my cock."

Her breath caught, but again she made no sign of protest. Getting onto her knees, she made her way toward me and then straddled my lap, rolling her hips up and down in a slow, torturous rhythm. One inch. Then two. Then out. Three inches, then four, then out. On and on, just a little deeper each time, wetting me with her juices, swallowing me bit by bit—until finally she gripped my base and pushed me so deep inside her my eyes nearly crossed from the sheer molten heat. If she was interested in getting to the finish line quickly, she didn't show it. Instead, she circled her arms around my neck and kept up her slow and steady pace, rising and falling slowly and pushing her breasts into my face with every stroke.

I cupped one in my hand, sucking a pink nipple until she gave me an approving squeeze and worked me faster, rewarding my tongue for its good work.

"You like that, baby," I murmured before taking her other nipple into my mouth and rolling the tip of my tongue around its peak. "Show me how much you like it."

Hell, did she ever. With her arms still circling my neck, she threw back her head and rolled her hips, taking just my throbbing head inside her as she dipped in short bursts and then longer, needier strokes, pounding over me. Slamming her hips down onto mine with a resounding *slap*. She was losing control—and fast. I gripped her ass, feeling the drag of her flesh against mine as she worked my shaft with her pussy.

"That's it, baby," I murmured, my voice husky with the need to come. "Let me feel you come again."

My balls drew up, but I closed my eyes, sucking her nipple still harder and willing myself to hold out for her. Her walls quaked and shuddered, and then I couldn't take it anymore. Grasping her hips firmly, I guided her up and down, impaling her with my cock in powerful thrusts until I was so deep inside her she ground out my name.

"Jackson, yes, Jackson, I'm going to—" Her words broke off, and she shook in my arms, her mouth falling open as she squeezed around me so tightly I couldn't hold back anymore. I slammed her hips down on mine again as we came together in greedy, gasping thrusts. Hot liquid spurted forward in a rush as wave after wave of pleasure crashed over me.

It was, hands down, the hottest sex of my life, and when she finally rolled from on top of me, I pulled off the condom with a sudden rush of disappointment. Not because the sex hadn't been amazing.

It had.

It had been so mind-blowing that I was already wishing we'd taken it slower or could do it again. But she was already standing on shaking legs, gathering up her clothes, and getting ready to go.

It should've made me happy. Hell, this was living the dream. Hook up with superhot funny girl. Have the best sex of my life. Walk away, no hard feelings, no strings, no drama, no bullshit.

Instead, I was actively resisting the urge to drag her back down on top of me and ask if she wanted to stay.

Amateur move, man, and you know it.

That kind of shit was what got a guy like me saddled with a woman who thought she was your girlfriend and tried to get you to go to her sister's wedding with her.

Not Piper, though. She was already dressed and slipping on her shoes.

"I... I should go. I'm just gonna get an Uber back to my car. But that was...um, thank you. That was exactly what the doctor ordered," she murmured, her cheeks a charming shade of pink.

She might look innocent, but this was a girl who knew the drill.

Perfect.

So why did part of me wonder why she was so eager to get away?

CHAPTER FIVE

PIPER

I had laid out my outfit the night before. Every last detail—my makeup, my jewelry—had all been planned to a T.

So why, then, did it all suddenly feel so wrong?

I stared into the mirror, wondering if the deep-crimson dress I wore hugged my curves a little too tightly or if the particular shade clashed with my auburn-colored hair. I'd opted for my glasses instead of contacts, and the thick, black frames I thought looked smart and trendy at the store now made me wonder if I looked more like Drew Carey than a sharp, capable professional.

Which, of course, was fine either way. I was going in for my first day of work, not planning a date.

My thoughts turned to my scorching-hot hookup from this past weekend.

And, damn, had it been hot.

Even now, when I should have been focusing on making a good impression and getting myself together, I found my mind drifting back to that night. No man had ever spoken to me that way—like I was the most desirable woman in the world. And the way he'd taken control of my body...like he knew better than I did how to make me feel good.

A shudder went through me, and I could feel my nipples go tight.

Shaking my head, I quickly yanked the red dress over my head and opted instead for the pair of nondescript black slacks on another hanger in front of me, pairing it with a sensible, white button-down shirt. I hooked my finger under the collar of a short, black jacket to match and called it good. True, the outfit made me look like a waiter, but it was just standard enough to be completely unnoticeable.

Perfect, polished, and professional. Just like I wanted to be.

Certainly nothing like the cheeky little tramp from the other night. My cheeks flushed again, and I forced thoughts of Jackson out of my mind one last time. It wasn't like I'd ever see him again, so what was the point in obsessing about it?

With a deep breath, I checked the time and grabbed my purse from the table by the door before making my way out of my apartment and onto the busy city street. My apartment was in the business district, not far from my new office building, so walking it was a nice way to take in the beautiful spring weather. Less nice was the constant swarm of perpetually irritated, stressed-out people who raced around the streets in this part of the city during the early morning rush, but I was nothing if not adaptable.

I pulled my planner from the front pocket of my purse, glanced down at the address again, and turned the corner with my head held high. Here, in this sea of busy-looking people, I wanted to feel like I fit in. To feel like I was ready to start a career as the right-hand woman to one of the most successful real estate moguls in the city.

I was cool and confident and strong. I was even the kind of woman who could have a random fling with a guy and head into work on Monday with a clear head.

I was independent and totally badass.

With these mantras running through my head, I stepped inside the building and beelined for the elevators. Straightening my Buddy Holly glasses, I pressed the button and forced a smiled as the set of doors in front of me slid open.

With quick strides, I boarded the elevator and then closed my eyes and waited for the doors to clang shut again and carry me off to my fresh new start. Before they did, however, I heard the soft thump of feet against the floor, so I opened my eyes to greet the stranger who joined me.

When I opened my mouth, though, I found my throat had completely gone dry. Blood rushed to my head.

This could not be happening.

After all the good work I'd done to get him out of my head, there he was, standing right in front of me.

Jackson, my "date" from the other night, selected his floor with the same cool confidence I'd felt only moments before. That, however, was long gone. In fact, it was so far gone I couldn't seem to remember what it felt like anymore. My knees were rubber, and I wobbled where I stood, overcome by the powerful memory of exactly what had happened the last time this man had entered my life...and my vagina.

Hysterical laughter threatened to bubble from my lips, and I bit my bottom one, hard. Maybe if I didn't make eye contact and just kept my trap shut, he wouldn't notice me. After all, with my business suit and glasses, who knew? Superman seemed to get by playing Clark Kent without a problem.

He turned, though, and met my gaze with instant recognition. For a split second, I thought his face might have betrayed that same shock I knew had to be plainly displayed on mine, but then his features smoothed and he said coolly, "Piper, nice to see you. I didn't realize you worked here."

I shook my head. "I don't. Or, you know, I didn't. I'm just..." I swallowed, trying to regain my bearings. What was it about this guy that made all my words come out in fluent Idiot?

"Today is my first day," I added lamely.

"Congratulations." He nodded. "I'm sure you'll like it here."

"I'm sure," I agreed.

For a long moment, neither of us said a word. Instead, we stared at each other, both apparently at a loss for what to say. In truth, I didn't know if I ought to have apologized for leaving the way I had after our night together. And, if I was being even more painfully honest, deep, deep down, I was harboring a pathetic and ill-advised hope that he might want to ask me out again.

But no. He stood there, looking at me. Seeing through me and making me feel just as raw and exposed as he had that night in the bar...and later.

My cheeks burned, and I glanced at the floor as the elevator dinged and slowed to a stop. Five. I was going to fifteen. But then, if I got off here, I could catch the next elevator and be free of him.

"This is me," I muttered and then clutched my purse a little tighter and scurried from the car as another woman took my place and nodded to Jackson.

"Mr. Dane," she murmured, and my ears pricked up.

Eyes wide, I spun around, but the elevator doors were closing as my breath caught in my chest.

Mr. Dane?

As in *the* Mr. Dane?

The CEO and owner of this company?

Mr. Dane, who also happened to be my new boss?

There had to be some mistake. Maybe it was a family-run business and Jackson had a brother or father who was in charge. Yes, that had to be it.

Heart beating out of my chest, I pressed the elevator button again. When the next one arrived, I climbed in, joining a group of weary-eyed workers. Nobody bothered to greet me as I stepped on, and I followed their lead, too tied up into knots to speak anyway.

Still, as the elevator climbed floors and people stepped off to start their day, my knees weakened. I tried to convince myself that surely karma couldn't be this cruel. Besides, a guy like Jackson couldn't be the CEO of this company.

He had the cockiness for the job, for sure, but he wasn't old enough. Guys like Mr. Dane—my boss—would have spent their entire lives building up an empire like this. A thirty-something guy could never manage such a feat. Not on this scale. No matter how cocky or good-looking he was.

The doors dinged, and I glanced at the numbers before stepping off and glancing around. The floor was filled with cubicles as far as the eye could see, and at the very end of the room was a huge office with wide, glass walls. The blinds of the room were closed, and I hitched my purse a little higher on my shoulder before starting for my destination.

As I walked, nobody in their cubicles turned to look at me. I focused on my mission, all the while doing my damnedest to convince myself that when I did knock on that door, Jackson would not be the man to answer it.

I inhaled deeply, lifted my hand, and knocked carefully, holding my breath as heavy footfalls sounded on the carpet. And then the door swung open to reveal him. My new boss. And the hottest fuck of my life.

Jackson Dane.

Just kill me now.

And he was staring at me in a way that left no doubt he was remembering every second of our night together.

Heat rose to my cheeks, and I glanced around him, hoping against hope that he'd merely been in the office talking to his superior. But I knew that wasn't the case. Because in this office?

Jackson *was* the superior.

"I think there's been a mistake," I spluttered. "The HR department hired me and told me I'd be Mr. Dane's new assistant, but I think they gave me the wrong person. Should I go to the office and—"

"There was no mistake," he said with a clipped nod. "I'm in need of a new assistant, and it looks like the HR department picked you. What a coincidence."

I shook my head. "The odds of that are—"

"Yes." He looked so damn calm. In fact, he didn't even seem surprised by this turn of events.

How could he do that? How could he pretend this wasn't the weirdest, most off-putting thing that had ever happened in the history of time?

"I'm sorry. Umm, this is super awkward. I'll just stop by HR and tell them to find someone else. This is clearly a bad idea." I spun on my heel to head back toward the elevators, my heart still pounding.

Damn it all.

I'd needed this job. My savings were beginning to dwindle, and if I didn't fix that soon, I was going to have to ask Hailey for money. And that would be a fate worse than death. If she thought she could boss me around now, she'd be insufferable if she also had me under her thumb financially.

Still, how could I work with a guy who looked at me the way Jackson did? Like I was the final course in the world's most indulgent meal? How could I file and schedule and organize for a man when, every time I bent down, I knew he could imagine every last detail of what was happening beneath my slacks?

I couldn't. It was wrong. But more than that—it was too tempting.

I took the first step of my walk of shame back to the elevator, when his deep voice rumbled.

"Piper, wait." A large hand closed around my bicep and spun me around so fast I nearly stumbled.

Blinking, mouth agape as I struggled for air, I found myself staring into Jackson's penetrating gaze. I shook my head. "Look, don't feel bad. There is really no reason to drag this out and—"

"I'm not doing it because I feel bad." He blew out a sigh and dragged a hand over his square jaw. "I looked at your résumé," he said, preempting my question.

"Okay," I said. "And?"

"I need you. You can't go. I haven't had a truly experienced assistant in months, and I desperately need one." There wasn't a hint of pleading in his voice, but I could tell he meant every word he said. "Look, the company is about to take on a major acquisition, and we're going through a huge merger. I need help. I can't wait for another assistant. Especially another one as qualified as you. If you can be professional, I can be professional. We're two adults. I don't see what happened between us being a problem."

I blinked again.

Seriously? After all the panting and moaning and sweating and grinding and...everything else we'd done together? He wanted me to work side by side with him?

Even now, my throat was threatening to close at the thought.

Had it really meant so little to him...been so run-of-the-mill that he could see me and not be completely accosted by the memory of our time together, like I was?

Damn. Talk about a reality check.

"Please, Piper, I need the help and you need a job. Don't walk away."

I considered him for a long moment. The right decision was to leave, I'd known it from the second I'd seen him on the elevator. But instead my mouth made an executive decision because, just like the other night, I couldn't seem to say no to this man.

"Fine, we'll give it a try," I said, not believing I was actually going to stay.

"Excellent." He offered me a clipped nod, looking, for all intents and purposes, like he'd never even considered another response out of me. The thought only solidified my new theory.

I wasn't the only one who couldn't say no to him. I was more sure than ever that it was a word he wasn't used to hearing much from anyone.

"Let's get started," he said, gesturing toward his office.

His gaze lingered on me, studying me and seeing through me the way he had the last time I'd seen him. For a brief second, I saw a flash of that carnal heat I'd seen in his eyes when we'd first met.

And in the space of that one tiny fraction of a second?

I knew I'd just made the biggest mistake of my life.

CHAPTER SIX

JACKSON

"The previous assistant left you a manual that you'll find waiting for you on your desk. I'll be in meetings all morning, so it should give you plenty of time to look over the materials and make sure you don't have any questions." I glanced at her from the corner of my eye, but she was too busy staring at the floor to bother looking at me.

Then again, she could have just been looking away in the interest of self-preservation. And after all, who could blame her? Even in the bellboy outfit she was wearing, I couldn't help but feel the urge to pull her to me right then and there and rip her clothes off.

It had to be something chemical, something purely scientific that made me feel this way. Like my testosterone could sense her pheromones or something. Either that or the fact that she'd been the best damn lay I'd had in my life.

My groin ached at the memory even now, and God only knew how the next few days might start to wear away at my resolve. If she bent over to file something in front of me and her skirt was short enough...

I flexed my jaw, fighting the urge to crowd her against the

wall and bury my face between those full, round tits she was working so hard to hide behind the shapeless shirt and jacket.

In spite of my words, I had no intention of keeping her on. It would be an untenable situation during a time where I needed to focus most on my business. Still, I had a mountain of shit to get through this week, and there was no way I was going to be able to replace her quickly. In fact, judging by Sally's tone the last time we talked, I was fairly certain it was going to be a real bitch trying to get her to find me more applicants. Until I was able to do that and get someone else in place—preferably someone old with warts and facial hair—I would find Piper another position in the company.

One that wasn't directly under me.

Even that thought sent another rush of blood to my cock. I blew out a sigh.

It was all going to work out fine. It was only for a few days. We'd get through it, and in the end, she'd still have a job. And me?

I'd be a free man again. Free to walk the halls without adjusting my suit jacket in an attempt to cover my raging hard-on.

Heading from my office, I noticed as each of my employees turned to nod and greet me. In my peripheral vision, I saw Piper grin at each of them, offering a little wave. I didn't bother to stop and introduce her. She wouldn't be here long enough to make friends. Instead, I slowed to a stop by her desk.

"This is you. You'll find what you need in the manual. The directives should be clear and to the point, but if you have questions..."

I trailed off, because frankly, I didn't care if she had questions. All I wanted was for her to be able to muddle through well enough to take even a little heat off me and keep me organized until someone more appropriate took her place.

I gestured to a black binder on her desk and then slipped into my office and closed the door, careful to make sure she'd taken her seat before making my way to my own desk. As usual, papers littered the surface, and I groaned as I opened my email to find a shit ton of new messages, each more important or serious than the last.

With the merger approaching, we had to ensure that every last one of the commercial listings we were acquiring was fit to come on board with us. We needed nothing but homers here, properties we could move quickly and sell at a premium. Which, in addition to being a major pain in the ass in general, meant that I was hearing from lawyers and accountants on a near constant basis these days.

My calendar, too, was covered with Post-it notes and crossed-out reminders in so many colors and handwritings that I couldn't be sure what was important and what wasn't.

Sighing, I glanced at the clock, pressed the buzzer, and waited for Piper to answer.

"How can I help you, Mr. Dane?"

"Coffee, please. I take it—"

"Black," she finished. "All in the manual. I'm a fast reader. I'll have it for you right away."

I blinked but then released the intercom button and focused back on my messages. Within a matter of two minutes, there was a soft knock and then the door swung open, revealing

Piper holding my favorite mug and walking slowly toward my desk.

"Here we go, and—" She gasped as she set down my coffee and then pressed a hand to her mouth, her beautiful eyes wide with dismay.

She pulled her hand from her mouth and cleared her throat. "I'm sorry, I didn't mean to be quite so dramatic, but...is this how your office always looks?"

She squinted at my multicolored Post-its and the utter chaos of my desk.

"Is there a problem?" I asked.

"It's just...how do you work like this?" She poked a faded Post-it whose words weren't even visible anymore.

"There's a system," I said coolly. There wasn't, but I wasn't about to let her walk in and start judging me. Who worked for whom here? "I figure it out."

"And what exactly is the system?" she asked, the doubt plain on her face.

"I figure it out." I shrugged. It hadn't always been this way. In fact, before my long-term assistant Imelda had retired, things had been shipshape all the time. Once she'd retired, though, I just hadn't been able to find anyone to replace her, and things had devolved.

Now, as I glanced around me, really seeing it for the first time, I barely suppressed the urge to wince. I could see that it might look a little overwhelming from the outside looking in.

My gaze took in the walls with notes taped to them.

Fuck, who was I kidding? It was like *A Beautiful Mind* up in here.

Still, something about the horror on Piper's face made me bristle, so I stood my ground.

"Eventually, as my assistant, you'd be responsible for getting this all digitized and keeping me on track."

"Of course," she said with a nod, her gaze flitting around the space like she was already mentally tidying up. "Well, you have a meeting in the conference room in five minutes. I've set up the projector and the computer in there, so you should be all set for the presentation."

"You did all that already?"

"Well, what else was I going to do while the coffee brewed?" She shrugged. "Do you mind if I work on your calendar a little while you're gone?"

"Knock yourself out," I said. Then I collected my papers and made my way to the meeting.

The presentation was short and sweet—just an update on where we stood in terms of the upcoming merger and a few housekeeping notes on the properties the company had acquired in the past few months. It was all straight and to the point, and by the time my coffee was finished, it was over.

An hour later, I headed back to my office and stopped short, looking around in confusion. Had I been so distracted that I'd gone to the wrong floor or something? I peered around the door to find Piper there in the corner with a sticky note in hand.

Okay, so, definitely my office, but it had been altered.

Completely.

Rather than facing the door, my desk was now focused on the one wall that wasn't glass. On that white wall hung four matching bulletin boards, each of which looked important and organized. My desk was completely cleared, save my computer and three boxes marked In, Pending, and Out, and the bar cart in the corner nearest the window had been replaced with a mini coffee maker.

Piper hovered near a board that had been marked off into three sections. She was thumbtacking a Post-it to it when I closed the door behind me. She looked up with a nod.

"Hi there."

"What the hell did you do?" I demanded, still in shock as I took one cautious step toward my desk.

"A few things, actually. First of all, studies show the workplace tends to be happier if there is fresh air and sunlight, so I adjusted the layout of the office to maximize productivity and mood."

I blinked. I guess I couldn't exactly argue with that. Still, though...

"What's all this, then?" I motioned to the boards.

"These are your new lifelines." She made a flourishing motion like she was Vanna White. "This"—she motioned to the board beside her—"is your Kanban board. Are you familiar with it?"

I'd heard of it, but I shook my head, waiting for her to continue.

"So, we have three sections. Things that need to be done, things you are doing, and things that have been done. This way, your to-do list doesn't clog up your brain. Beneath it, I've made another Kanban board of things you'd like me to do, so rather than sending emails and forgetting whether you've told me things, they'll all be directly visible to both of us."

"Makes sense, I guess," I said somewhat grudgingly. "And everything else?"

"Your calendar." She moved to the next board. "That's been color-coded based on who you're meeting with. Personal matters are in black for quick reference, but I posted a key for everything else." She smiled. "You also have a digital version on your computer now that will remind you of events the day and hour before."

"And my bar cart?" I asked. I knew I was being an asshole, because so far everything she said made perfect sense, but change and I were like oil and water, and I was still reeling from the unapproved total office renovation.

She'd said she wanted to move things around a little, not change everything.

"It says in your manual that you drink five cups of coffee a day and hardly ever drink in the office. Makes no sense to have a bar cart where there could be a hot, fresh cup of coffee at arm's length."

Even now, my mouth watered for a fresh mug, but that wasn't the point. "The champagne—"

"Is for clients." She nodded. "So I've put it in the executive break room and will fetch it on request. Which, as far as I can tell, happens like twice a month. This way, we can chill the bottles on ice before clients arrive. I've set up a system."

"That's an understatement," I said, glancing around. "But if you've set up all this stuff for me to do myself, then what are you going to do?"

"Help you with all the other stuff you have to do," she said with a strained smile. "That's what you hired me for."

"Right." I scrubbed a hand over my face and then settled into my chair. "Thank you. Will you please—"

"Lunch is already ordered."

I shook my head. "How did you know?"

"Same time every day." She shrugged. "Says so in the manual. I had your Meals-to-Go login, so I've gotten you the usual at Sal's Deli. It should be here right on schedule."

"I hope you ordered something for yourself," I said, though in truth I felt lost for words.

She nodded, her tone clipped and businesslike. "Yep, you gave me a very generous allowance for lunches, and I appreciate it."

Without a word, she turned on her heel and strolled toward the door. When it clicked shut behind her, I stared after her, wondering what the hell had just happened.

In the history of all my assistants, the first few days were nothing more than handholding and making sure they remembered how I liked my coffee. Never—not once—had anyone walked in and taken control like Piper. Nobody had ever been so thoughtful, so attentive.

Which, of course, made my life that much harder.

After all, I couldn't exactly get rid of a perfectly good assistant when it had taken me months to find someone like her. But then, even when she'd been explaining her perfectly color-coded system, I'd been half imagining unbuttoning that staid little shirt of hers and getting another look at what lay underneath.

A lethal combination of feelings, there was no doubt

about it.

Biting the inside of my cheek, I gripped the arms of my chair, propelled myself up, and walked toward my square of neat bulletin boards. Maybe she'd missed something— some detail that would ruin everything if I hadn't caught it myself. That would give me a reason to let her go with a clear conscience. After all, organization was good, but not at the cost of business.

But no. I examined the calendar, the to-do list, everything. Not a single thing had been misplaced—right down to my haircut on the eighteenth. She'd taken care of everything.

I glanced up at the ceiling and then trudged back to my desk and sat again. I had plenty to do. I had no business worrying about what I was going to do about this assistant. Still, a part of me felt like I should have known this was a bad idea.

Considering how attentive and responsive she'd been on that rooftop, there shouldn't have been a doubt in my mind that she'd be the same professionally. She did everything wholeheartedly—just like me.

I growled under my breath as I opened my emails and tried to focus on the many messages but found there was nothing for me to look at.

Nothing at all.

My inbox had been completely emptied.

Pressing the intercom, I waited as Piper said, "How can I help you, Mr. Dane?"

"What happened to all my emails?" I snapped.

"They've been coordinated to appear when you need

them. I cleaned out the junk mail and scheduled the rest. If you prefer to see them in total, just click the check box to the right of your inbox. I hope I didn't overstep...?"

"You—" I closed my eyes and then opened them again. If her email system was as foolproof as she said... I clicked the checkbox, and they all appeared. "No, you didn't. Thank you."

I released the button and glanced around the room again.

She was the world's best assistant. And the best lover I'd ever had. In fact, I'd spent my entire weekend replaying my night with her over in my mind and my entire Sunday night trying to convince myself I had the will power to stop myself from jerking off while thinking about her.

Surely having her here would be total hell.

Unless, of course, I could have the best of both worlds...

CHAPTER SEVEN

PIPER

"Tequila!" I shouted, both as an order to the bartender and in response to the catchy song blaring over the bar speakers.

I sipped the margarita in front of me, pushed my empty shot glass toward the edge of the bar, and then glanced around at my fellow businesspeople, all unwinding on Cinco de Mayo after a long day of work.

The past week had been a blur of activity and organization, but I was definitely falling into the swing of things. In fact, a few times, some of my officemates had stopped by my desk to offer their congratulations on my ability to "tame the dragon."

And after working with Jackson all week, I could definitely see why. His moods were changeable to say the least. Driven one minute and frustrated the next. Sometimes he would fall into a trance so deep that I was sure he didn't hear me when I spoke. But other times...

Other times, I knew he saw me. His gaze bore into me, and though I'd been careful to wear my drabbest business clothes, I was sure he was seeing right through them. That he could tell the way my nipples still stiffened to a straining peak whenever I set eyes on him. That he knew the way my knees weakened when he spoke. But more than that, I was sure he reveled in it.

A few times, he'd even called me into his office only to tell me to leave again, his question unasked. But I knew what the question was. I could see it in the tick of his jaw when he looked at me or the way he breathed in my perfume whenever I was near.

It had been so hard to leave that night on the rooftop. To walk away and not beg him to do it all over again. But I knew if I didn't, I'd be in deep. Too deep. He'd made it more than clear he wanted to hook up. A one-night thing and nothing more. Once he'd rocked my world—twice, no less—I hadn't needed much prompting to head for the hills. If I didn't and we did *that* again?

I might have dropped to one knee and asked for his hand in marriage.

Okay, not really, but still. He was addictive. I knew it from one taste. Which meant I had to stay away.

Only now there was no escape, was there?

The bartender set another shot in front of me, and with the memory of Jackson's dark eyes searing into me, I downed it in one and sipped my margarita as a chaser.

Tonight was not going to be about Jackson Dane. Truth be told, I already spent way too much time thinking about— and fantasizing over—him. No, tonight I was young and single in a new city and looking for someone to catch my eye.

Which, luckily, they did.

My gaze fell on a man staring me down across the bar, his red tie partially undone as he rolled the tip of his finger around his beer glass. He looked like a young professional, complete with the suit and slicked-back hair. The slightest bit of five o'clock shadow darkened his features, and I offered him a coy smile before turning my attention to my drink again.

He was handsome. Slightly out of character, maybe, but I had just enough liquid courage in me to consider crossing the bar and introducing myself.

As it was, though, I grabbed my phone from my pocket and did my best to squish down the fact that all I could think was how he wasn't quite as good-looking as Jackson. Didn't have that sparkle. That sexy charm that rolled off him in waves.

Not by a mile.

"Hey," rumbled a deep voice near my ear. I glanced up to find myself practically nose-to-nose with this new handsome stranger.

"I'm Steve. What's your name?"

"Oh. Hi, I'm Piper. Nice to meet you."

My phone blared a loud tinkling noise, and I glanced down to see *Jackson Dane* blinking across the screen.

I held up a finger, my heart pounding in my chest. "I have to take this. I'll be right back."

I rolled off my seat and scuttled quickly to the exit, pushing the door open with my hip.

Stepping outside the bar, I pressed the answer key and then held my phone to my ear. "Hello?"

"Piper, I need you to come into the office." Jackson's tone was matter-of-fact. As if every boss called their employees at seven o'clock on a Friday night.

"I really...can't," I said.

"On a date?" he asked, his tone clipped.

"No, not that it's any of your business," I added briskly. "It's after work hours, and I've had a couple of drinks."

"That doesn't matter. I don't mind, and I need you here ASAP. Won't take long. I'll see you shortly."

The line died, and I stared at my phone for a moment, trying to convince myself that he hadn't just ordered me around like some sort of indentured servant he'd smuggled here on a ship in the fifteen hundreds.

I shouldn't go. I shouldn't let him win.

But even as I thought over all the reasons it was wrong to go back into work tonight, I found myself paying my bill and making excuses to Steve before I hit the sidewalk and marched the two blocks to the dark-mirrored glass office tower where I worked.

I knew it was stupid, but dang it, I actually liked my job. I liked that Jackson needed me.

What else do you like, Piper?

I shoved the mocking voice away and willed the heat from my face. Sure, it was after hours, but I could be professional.

I entered the building after a janitor let me in, and I made for the elevator swiftly, closing my eyes to stop the slight sway of the world around me as I walked. I was one tequila shot away from hiccupping, but Jackson had robbed me of that. Or maybe he'd saved me. I wasn't quite sure.

Squaring my shoulders, I stepped from the elevator and made my way to his office, not bothering to knock before I opened the door and crossed my arms over my chest.

"What was so important that I had to come in on Friday night?"

He looked up at me—almost as if he was surprised I'd actually come—and then offered me half a begrudging smile.

"You look...nice."

"Oh, I—"

Shit.

I'd forgotten that I'd loosened up a little after work, pulling my hair from its staid bun and letting it fall around my shoulders. My button-down shirt had been unbuttoned to show the slightest hint of cleavage, and I'd changed from my usual slacks into a bright-red skirt that showed off my legs.

"You're sure you weren't on a date?" he asked, his laser-beam eyes looking through me.

I shook my head, trying not to read anything into the question. So he was nosy. No big.

"Positive. Once more, not that it's any of your business," I added again for good measure.

"I'm glad to hear that. Sit down." He motioned to one of the seats in front of him, and I took my place carefully, smoothing my skirt beneath me as I sat.

"You've been drinking," he asked, though it wasn't a question.

"As I said, yes." I pointed to the glass on his lacquered desk. "Apparently, I'm not the only one."

"No. I've had two myself." He folded his hands on his desk and regarded me with a thoughtful look. "But I want to make sure you have your wits about you."

"Why is that?" I asked.

"Because I have an important proposition for you." His gaze seared my skin, and I crossed my legs, once again feeling like he could see straight through my thin layer of clothing.

"Go on," I asked, nerves skittering through me like lightning.

"Before I tell you, you need to promise me you're sober enough to listen."

I gave him a single nod, not just because I was curious but because the second I'd laid eyes on him, I'd felt sober, though slightly drunk on him. He had that effect on me—of draining away all other outside forces and commanding all my attention in a way only he could.

"Good," he said. "Now, your performance here this week has been outstanding."

"Thank you," I murmured.

"No, thank you. I'm very impressed with your work. So much so that I am not willing to lose you as an assistant, so please keep that in mind as you consider what I'm offering you."

I frowned slightly. "Okay."

"I can't go on like this," he said simply.

"Like what?" I asked, blinking back at him.

"I can't work side by side with you while I have a constant erection."

I drew back, both surprised and sort of turned on by his forthrightness. "Oh."

"Every time I look at you, I imagine stripping off your clothes and fucking you right here on my desk. And now that I see you in that tiny red skirt...you have no idea how much I want to cross this desk and spread your legs apart so I can lick the space between your thighs."

I swallowed hard. "Mr. Dane—"

"Jackson," he corrected. "Ever since the first time I had you, I haven't stopped thinking about you, and I have to think there's a reason you're here now. I'm not interested in relationships, Piper. I don't have the time or the inclination. But I want you more than any other woman I've ever had. And the way your body fits with mine?" He shook his head. "It's no accident you're here, that's all I know."

"What are you trying to say?" I pressed, struggling to breathe as I imagined him sinking to his knees in front of me, pushing my legs apart, and having his way with me. Teasing my already aching bud again the way he did that night. Tasting him the way he'd tasted me.

"I'm trying to say that I want you. I want you as my assistant, and I want you in my bed."

"That's not possible." I shook my head, trying to fight back the primal urges willing me to straddle him then and there. To forget about what was smart and do what my body was begging me to do.

"And why not? I don't see why we can't keep it professional during the day and enjoy ourselves at night. I've put a lot of thought into this, and I know we can handle it, if you're willing."

"We'll be caught," I said, my voice barely above a whisper. If he only knew how willing I was. But God, would this be stupid. Foolhardy. Reckless.

"By whom? I'm the boss here." He shrugged. "I don't have shareholders I need to keep up appearances for. All I need to do is follow my own instincts, and all my instincts tell me this is something I can't ignore. I've spent all day thinking about you, even though you've been wearing those awful clothes to hide yourself from me. Tell me the truth. You've been thinking about me too."

I let out a shallow breath, nodding despite my better judgment.

Because, really, there was no denying it. I was sure he knew, could feel every time I'd come into his office and imagined splaying myself out in front of him. Every time I'd envisioned bending over the desk in front of me and staring out at the city skyline while he pushed into me over and over until I broke apart at his touch.

"See? So we're in agreement. We'll be casual sexual partners during non-work hours, and you will retain your position as my assistant during the day."

"We can't," I tried again, straining to hear the voice of dissent that was growing weaker and weaker in my mind. "What happens when one of us gets tired of the other?"

What I really meant was *What happens when you get tired of me?* Because I couldn't imagine ever tiring of him...

"Nothing. I think we're both smart and mature enough to look at what happened fondly and continue working together. You're an amazing assistant. Nothing has to change there. But this thing between us? It needs to run its course. It's meant to be, Piper. Do you need me to prove that to you?" He stood, his height dwarfing even the dark skyline behind him.

I shivered. "I don't know. I can't choose right here and now."

"Then let me give you something to help you weigh your options."

I should have stood right then and there. Should have gotten up and marched out the door without a second thought. But instead, I uncrossed my legs and stood, waiting as he circled the corner of his desk and crowded me until all I could feel was him—the smell of him, the heat of him, his overwhelming presence.

He was everything.

And I could do nothing to deny him.

CHAPTER EIGHT

JACKSON

As I stepped toward her, my pulse hammered in my wrists and my shaft ached with the memory of the last time we were together—just like it did every time I was around her. I approached, the familiar scent of her lavender and chamomile shampoo filling the air, and it was all I could do not to tell her to get on her knees in front of me right then and there.

But no, right now I had to convince her that we were meant to be lovers. It was my one and only mission. And I never failed a job.

Slowly, I pushed an errant strand of silken hair behind her ear and then twisted it around my finger.

"Don't you remember how good it was, Piper?" I asked, my voice deep and low. "When I sank between your thighs and licked you?"

She swallowed hard, and I cupped her cheek, stroking the pad of my thumb against her tight jaw.

"You tasted so good, you know that? Every time I see you, I think of that. How good you tasted. My tongue on your pretty pink clit."

She shivered, and my hand dropped lower, tracing the

column of her throat and then the hollow of her collarbone.

"And then, when I'm thinking about you? I think about how good it would be to taste the rest of you. To kiss my way down your neck..." I trailed my thumb up and down her throat again. "And your breasts..." I rested my palm just above the swell of her chest. "And your perfect little nipples."

She shivered again, her pupils dilating as she met my gaze. Her breath was coming faster now, and I knew I had her under my spell just as much as I was under hers.

"Do you know what I thought when I first saw you in this tiny red skirt?"

She shook her head, eyes wide, her gaze still trained on mine.

"I thought of how nice it would be to undress you until you weren't wearing anything but this skirt. And then you know what I'd do?"

She swallowed before shaking her head again.

"I'd grip the hem." I did exactly that, and she made no move to stop me, which only made my heart pound harder and my blood run hotter. "And I'd hike it all the way up to your waist so that I could see all of you. You know what I'd do next?"

She took a deep breath, her warm exhale fanning against my chest.

"I'd bend you over my desk and use your skirt to pull you into me while I slid my cock into you. Long and deep, over and over again."

I released the hem of the skirt and then made my way to the collar of her shirt, fingering the first button with a light caress. "So tell me, Piper. What do you want?"

"I want you to undress me, and I want to undress you," she said without missing a beat.

Excellent.

It wasn't an answer to my earlier proposal, but it was something. I'd get to be inside her one more time.

"That can be arranged." I unfastened the top button on her shirt and then worked the rest deftly until the two sides slid apart to reveal a pretty purple bra with little lace detailing. When I was finished, she shrugged from the shirt and reached for mine, making quick work of my tie before unfastening the buttons with enviable speed.

Grabbing the hem of her skirt, I hiked it up exactly as I'd promised and glimpsed the scrap of matching purple panties beneath. At the sight of them, I wanted to sink to my knees and drag them down with my teeth, but Piper distracted me as she reached for my belt and unfastened it quickly before pulling down my fly and dropping to the floor as she lowered my pants.

Carefully, I stepped from my slacks and gripped the desk on either side of me as she guided me back, her knees spread apart ever so slightly as she settled onto the ground just as I'd imagined so many times.

My throbbing length bucked and jerked in anticipation of those soft fingers...that molten mouth.

With one delicate hand, she gripped the elastic of my boxers and pulled them down, allowing my member to jut out in front of her.

"When you think of me, do you touch yourself?" she asked, her voice breathy, needy, and even now, a bit shy.

I nodded and then gripped the base of my shaft to

demonstrate. Instead, though, she pushed my hand aside and replaced it with her own, working me up and down as she stared up at me, teasing me with her tantalizing plump lips so near.

"Do you think of me when you touch yourself?" I asked, the question alone making me ache with another swell of longing.

At first, I didn't think she was going to answer. But then she looked me dead in the eyes and nodded, wetting her lips.

"Yes."

She gripped me harder, working me slightly faster before leaning in closer and licking my head with one long, beautiful stroke of that tongue.

Looking up at me all the while, she closed her mouth over me, bobbing up and down as she worked the rest of me with her hand, and I let out a little groan as the tip of her tongue stroked me up and down in time with her movements.

"Fuck," I ground out, and I felt her smile around me as she let out a little moan of approval.

The vibration of her voice sizzled through me, rocking me to my core. I fisted her hair, letting her control the movements, fighting the desire to rush it. To plunge forward and feel the tender flesh at the back of her throat.

She must have sensed my need, because she increased the suction, her cheeks going concave as she drew on my stiff cock, sucking harder, deeper, until I knew I couldn't take another moment. If I had my way, we'd be able to take it slow the next time or the next after that. Right now, I was like a wild man, desperate to be inside her.

Gripping her hair in my hand, I guided her back until she released me.

"That's enough. Now it's my turn." Taking her shoulders in both hands, I pulled her back to standing and then gripped her panties and broke the delicate string with a *snap*. The scrap of fabric tumbled to the floor, and she looked down at it for a moment before her hungry gaze found mine again.

"Those are mine now," I said.

She gave me another wide-eyed stare and a nod, and I bent over to pull a condom from my pocket before rolling it over my waiting shaft. Eyes locked on mine, she slid onto the desk, spread her legs apart to show me every inch of her pretty pink center.

"You coming?"

It took all my effort not to drop down in front of her and lick the space long and deep until she came, but I knew I couldn't wait that long. I had to have her—and soon.

"No," I growled and then pulled her from the surface of the desk and flipped her around before wrenching her skirt back up to her waist. "You had your fun. Now we do things my way."

"And what if I want to do things my way?"

"Then you'll have to come back for more, I guess." Her bare ass was round and smooth, and I squeezed my eyes closed because suddenly it was all too much.

"You ready for me?" I asked, my throat so tight with need that I could barely squeeze the words out.

She nodded, and I gripped myself hard before pushing into her wet, waiting heat.

God, how I'd fantasized about this moment—having her here, bent over my desk with the whole city in front of us. I could see my reflection in the wide glass window, standing over her, entering her slow and steady. But all my fantasies and reflections couldn't compare to the actual feel of her.

She was soft and pliable in my hands, leaning into me as I slid deep and then deeper until I was buried to the hilt. Gripping her skirt with one hand, I pulled her still deeper, and she let out a little satisfied moan.

"Say my name, Piper," I murmured.

"Jackson," she moaned, arching back against me.

My shaft hardened to the point of pain, and she used her inner muscles to squeeze me even tighter, encouraging me to ride her faster. But I couldn't. The second I lost my self-control, I would be bucking into her so hard and fast that everything would skitter from my desk and she'd be gripping the mahogany edges for dear life. We'd be done before we even started.

No, I had to take my time, working her body nice and slow before I took everything she had to offer.

So, with a firm grip on her skirt, I took my other hand and smacked the tender curve of her ass, loving the little yelp she let out as much as the moan of pleasure when I soothed her, kneading the skin gently with my palm.

"Do you like it, Piper?" I asked.

Smack.

"Mmm-hmm," she murmured, arching her back into my hand as I massaged the space again.

With every playful blow, her channel tightened still more

around me, but I held back, no matter how hard it was to continue my slow, steady rhythm.

Smack.

I rubbed her reddening skin, and she whimpered her approval.

"Please, Jackson, I want everything," she said. "I'm so close. Just please, fuck me."

Her words pushed me over the edge, and my balls went tight as hot liquid snaked up my shaft. Gripping her hips tight, I pulled back and plunged forward.

Instantly, her walls quaked around me, and she clutched the edge of the desk as her body writhed with pleasure. And then, when her voice broke into a chorus of whimpers, it was all over.

Gripping her skirt with both hands, I thrust into her harder and faster, ignoring the sharp squeaks of the desk as I took her in the deep, dirty way I'd been imagining all week.

"Yes, Jackson," she cried, and I gripped her hair in one hand, pulling gently as she gasped and slapped the surface of the desk. Looking at our reflection, I could see the pure ecstasy in her eyes as I pushed deeper with every thrust until my cup of pens skittered to the floor and she knocked my papers down along with them.

"Lose control for me again, baby," I ground out, and she did, squeezing me so tight that stars shot in front of my eyes while my balls drew up and the coil of tension low in my stomach expanded and, at last, collapsed, shooting waves of pleasure through my body with so much force that I let out a low groan as I pushed into her again and again.

Then it was over and I was shooting into her hard and fast, cursing the damn condom that separated me from her. It was so good, so hot, so intense that I knew this wouldn't—*couldn't*—be the last time.

CHAPTER NINE

PIPER

I'd never look at mahogany the same way again.

Even now, walking home from the office, my cheeks burned with the memory of how Jackson had bent me over the desk and laid into me.

Swallowing hard, I straightened my skirt, irrationally sure that everyone who passed me on the street would be able to smell the sex on me. That they would somehow know exactly what—and who—I'd done. And if they could?

Then they would know, like I knew, that I was the biggest idiot who'd ever lived.

I fumbled for my keys as I reached my apartment complex and then made my way inside and ignored the unsteady click of my shoes on the linoleum floors as I headed toward the elevators.

What had I been thinking? Of course my natural inclination might have been to blame my alcohol-addled mind, but that was no use. The second I'd heard Jackson's voice on the phone, I'd been stone-cold sober. And when I'd heard what he had to say...

I reached my door and made quick work of the lock before

making a beeline for my bed. I needed to lie down, to sleep away what I'd done and forget it ever happened. Who knew? Maybe when I woke up tomorrow, all of this was just some bad dream.

Except, of course, it wasn't bad.

It would have been better—ideal, even—if it had been bad.

Instead, it was perfect. Jackson had worked my body like a fine-tuned machine, and again I was left with another memory to haunt me as I tried to work side by side with him. How would I be able to look at his hands without remembering the way he'd held my hips, hard and commanding? Without the searing memory of his hips slapping against my ass, mingling the pain with my pleasure and heightening both in the process.

I couldn't. Just like I couldn't look at his lips without remembering the way they burned against my mouth, the way his tongue stroked mine and coaxed out every begging moan in my body.

Another ache rose between my thighs, and I squeezed them together, fighting the urge to call him and ask for round two—or was it three now?

No matter the number, it couldn't happen again, no matter what kind of promises he made. When things like that happened in an office, it was only an amount of time before others in the office found out. I wasn't willing to be the gossip around the water cooler, not for him and not for anyone.

My dignity was simply too important to me.

Breathing deep, I closed my eyes, grabbed a pillow, and shoved it over my face. I couldn't undo what had been done. I couldn't go back and force myself not to be swept away by his filthy, tantalizing promises. But I could promise myself that it wouldn't happen again.

And that was exactly what I was going to do. On Monday, I was going to march into his office and own up to the mistake I'd made. I'd tell him I was sorry if he thought I'd led him on by sleeping with him, but it had been a moment of weakness. I'd tell him what happened had meant nothing to me.

Which it did, of course. It had meant nothing to me. Nothing at all.

If he fired me? Well, I'd faced the challenge of joblessness before, hadn't I?

And if he didn't...

I'd find a way to live with the memory of his warm, muscled body pressing into mine and spurring me toward release.

I shoved the pillow harder against my face and debated screaming into it, but before I got the chance, the muffled sounds of something jangly and bright sounded from the floor beside me.

My phone.

Maybe it was Jackson, calling to tell me he didn't want to go through with his proposition. That he'd thought it through, and now that he'd had me again, he had decided against it.

Lord knows I hadn't given him a chance to say much when I'd run out of the office like it was on fire after we'd made love.

I snatched my purse from the floor, dug out my phone, and pressed it to my ear, not bothering to check the ID before answering.

"Hello?" I said, realizing with a wince that my voice was breathy and anything but casual.

"Hey, are you okay? You sound like I caught you in the middle of...something." There was a note of amusement in Hailey's voice, and I shook my head before realizing she obviously couldn't see me.

"Um, no, no, I'm fine. What's up?"

"Not a whole lot. Just calling to see how work has been this past week? I've barely heard from you."

"Oh, right, yeah. It's fine."

"Fine? That's it? You're the only person I know who can talk about their job for more than five minutes without wanting to hang themselves. Do you hate it or something?"

"No, no." I chewed on the inside of my cheek, but when I didn't say anything else, Hailey pressed on.

"You didn't tell me how your date went either, you know. I'm starting to think you're cutting me out of your life."

"No, uh, it was fine."

"Fine again, huh?" Hailey accused. "All right, what gives?"

"Nothing. What's with the third degree?"

"I know you better than this, that's all. I'm not buying the act. I don't know who you are, but my sister would be shouting at me from here to high heaven about setting her up on a date instead of a casual friend meetup like she asked."

A note of anger flared in my chest at the memory. "I never said I was happy about what you did, but if I yelled at you for every time you didn't listen to me, I would have shouted myself hoarse a long time ago."

"Ah, that sounds a little more familiar," she said with a snort. "Now spill. What's going on that you aren't telling me?"

I could have—and probably should have—lied. She never

would have known the truth. But still, I couldn't bring myself to do it.

"Just things at work are a little more complicated than I'd planned."

"For you?" Hailey practically choked. "Between all your organizational systems? What could possibly be getting in the way?"

"That date you set me up on, actually," I replied waspishly.

"He sent something to you at work or something?" she asked, sounding perplexed but interested.

"No, uh...he's my boss." I tried to play it off as chill as possible, but there was a long pause on the line, and then Hailey spoke again, slowly and carefully.

"Well, that shouldn't be such a big deal either. You went on one date with the guy. I don't see what's—"

"I slept with him." I forced the words out, and then, weighing my options, I added, "Plus, I just slept with him again about ten minutes ago."

"Oh. Em. Gee. Finally. I've been waiting for this day to come," she squealed with glee. "Pop the champagne; you broke a rule."

"Not technically. He's the one who makes the rules, and he said..." I shook my head, trying to think of what he'd said that I was willing to repeat aloud. "He said since he's the boss, it wouldn't be such a bad thing for us to be casual lovers."

"*Casual lovers?*" Hailey repeated. There was no disguising the excitement in her voice now. I hung my head, waiting for her to settle down before I continued.

"So, he doesn't want to date; he just wants to screw your

brains out," she added matter-of-factly.

I winced. "He didn't exactly put it that way, but that was the general idea."

"Well, what did you say?" Hailey pressed.

"I said no."

"Except you also slept with him, so...sort of still up in the air, isn't it?"

"You don't understand. The way the guy looks at me... I can't even form words. My heart starts going, and then before I know it he's pulling off my clothes and—" I stopped short, catching myself.

"And what!" Hailey squeaked.

"Maybe you're the one who needs a boyfriend. I'm not telling you the sordid details of my affair with my boss."

"Be that as it may, it looks like you have a choice to make."

"And I've made it. He's not going to fire me if I say no. We'll just have to find a way to work together."

"So the sex was bad?" Hailey asked.

"No, the sex was..." I shook my head. "The sex was none of your business."

"I'm just trying to understand."

"He's my boss. What else is there to understand?"

"Well, if you're not the girl getting the flowers, you're going to be the one sending them, right?"

I paused. "What do you mean?"

"Guys like that don't pine. He's not going to sit around. High-powered businessmen are going to get what they want, and if he's not going to get it from you, he's going to get it somewhere else. So tell me, are you going to be okay as the woman scheduling his dates with other women?"

"Yeah, I..." I started, but I couldn't say it.

In my mind, I could convince myself the sex had been exactly that—a frantic, urgent need we'd both raced to satisfy. But in truth? Knowing another woman would feel the callouses on his hands and hear the filthy things he said...the words that should have been directed at me?

"But what if people find out about us and talk about us around the office?"

"The important man who has a beautiful secretary? Wake up, kid, they're going to talk about you regardless of what you do," Hailey said.

"What if... What if I start to care about him, though? He's not the kind of guy who's going to stick around. I could be setting myself up for heartbreak."

"Every time you get involved with someone, you're setting yourself up for heartbreak. So tell me, isn't walking away now still going to set yourself up for disappointment?" she asked flatly.

Her words rang in my ears, and I let out a deep breath I hadn't realized I'd been holding.

"I guess I have a lot to think about," I said.

"Sounds like it. But you do have the benefit of knowing that you can handle anything, and I'll always be here."

"Thanks, Hail." We said goodbye shortly after that, though I couldn't remember whatever else we talked about. Instead, my brain was reeling with scenarios of what I might do on Monday when I walked into the office.

Jackson would want his answer, and I'd need to have one

for him.

Still, even after everything, it felt like I was sliding down the track to disaster. On one hand, I ordered flowers for other women and lived a life without ever knowing Jackson's touch again. On the other, I had Jackson, with no guarantee that his decisive, dark eyes wouldn't burn a deep, unhealable hole in my heart.

But then, I'd come to the city to start my life over. To try fresh, new things.

Taking a chance on the city's most devious playboy... What could be more exciting?

Or more painful...

CHAPTER TEN

JACKSON

It was too damn early, even for my standards.

As I walked through the dark hall toward my office, the automatic lights flickered to life. I rubbed my eyes, stifling the yawn I'd been holding since I woke up that morning. I'd slept like shit, just like I had on Friday and Saturday, and if I didn't get a cup of coffee soon, I was sure I'd collapse right here on the drab beige carpet.

Stepping into my office, I made quick work of setting up my one-cup coffee maker and booting up my laptop. Through my windows, the lavender-salmon dawn was starting to light the spring sky, and a deep tinge of red ran through the clouds like blood.

But then, ever since Friday night, it felt like I saw the same shade of red everywhere I went. It was on my dishes and in street signs. The color of stoplights and even my car. All of it matched the damn tiny skirt Piper had been wearing on Friday night—the skirt I'd yanked up to her waist and used as an anchor as I thrust into her over and over again.

My groin throbbed at the memory, and I took another step toward my brewer, where I grabbed my mug and took a long sip. Every time I'd closed my eyes all weekend long, I'd been assaulted by the memory of what Piper and I had done—the way her pliable little body had submitted to my will.

A few times, I'd even been tempted to call her and demand an answer to my proposition. But I couldn't, and wouldn't, show that kind of weakness.

The truth was she was going to give me one of two answers—either she would agree to casually screw me on the side or she wouldn't. Her choice ought to have made no difference to me. After all, it wasn't like there was a shortage of women who wouldn't jump at that arrangement.

But fuck, it just did. It mattered to me—immensely.

Still, that didn't change the fact that when I tried to close my eyes at night, it was with the mental image of Piper climbing on top of me and riding me hard and rough while her breasts bounced and her wild hair fell loose around her shoulders.

Pushing the thought away, I took another sip of my coffee, settled at my computer, and tried to focus on work. The merger was getting closer every day, and God only knew I had plenty to do before then. Everyone else in the office building would start pouring in in an hour or so, and it would help to get a head start on things before the administrative meeting that was to take place first thing this morning.

I glanced at the variety of boards Piper had laid out for me and then opened my email and scanned for her name. Nothing. I checked my phone, but there were no new messages. Not one.

At least that would make it easier to concentrate.

I opened the first email and scanned it quickly, but before I could tap out my reply, I glanced at the corner of my desk and stopped. The picture frame that normally sat there was gone. I blinked, wondering what might have happened, but then, in another flash, I remembered the clatter of it falling to the ground as Piper gripped the end of the desk, her body bumping against the lacquered top.

It would be on the floor. Wheeling over, I bent to pick it up and set it right, and then shook my head and tried to focus again on the message opened in front of me. In the corner of my eye, I could see a few people already starting to shuffle in as more lights flickered into existence.

I swallowed hard.

Okay, back to work.

A notification popped up in the corner of my monitor, and I clicked on it to find a reminder about the administrative meeting. Piper had linked her calendar with my own, and I could see that she would be there as well.

The rest of her day, like mine, was busy, and I spotted a small window of time between the administrative meeting and her lunch break that looked tantalizingly free. Clicking on the empty space, I typed instructions to her to meet me in the lounge of the hotel around the corner.

It was presumptuous, I knew that, and it was more than enough for her to sue me for sexual harassment if things didn't go my way...

But damn if I could focus on that when every time I looked at my own desk, it was with the memory of her breasts pressed against the counter as I worked her from behind. No, when it came to Piper, I had to take risks, and today I was going to take the biggest one of all.

I snatched up my laptop, made my way to the conference room, and waited until one by one, the other assistants from around the office building filed in. Each of them glanced at me curiously as they entered with their coffee and tea, but other than the odd good morning, none of them bothered to question me.

Not that I could blame them for their wondering expressions. In all the years since I'd opened this branch of the company, I'd never once bothered to show up to these meetings. But today was different—for more reasons than one.

Sally, my HR nemesis, entered the room and offered me a warm smile for once, probably because I hadn't fired my new assistant yet. But as she greeted me, my peripheral vision snagged on the one person I'd been waiting to see.

Piper was walking into the room, her shoulders hitched high around her ears as she fidgeted with the papers in her arms. Today she was wearing one of her usual staid outfits—a white button-down shirt with a sensible olive skirt—and her wild hair was pulled into a tight bun at the nape of her neck.

It didn't bode well for what I was hoping she had to tell me, but after I extended a cheerful "good morning" to Judy from Human Resources, I opened my computer and got down to business.

With the clearing of her throat, Judy started the meeting, and I listened quietly and intently until someone from the finance department got up and launched into a diatribe at the end of the table.

Then, opening the messenger on my computer, I typed out:

J Dane: *Good morning*

For a long moment there was no answer, and then three little dots appeared, letting me know someone had seen my message and was responding to it. I glanced at her from the corner of my eye, studying as she typed and deleted and then typed and deleted again before finally sending:

P Daniels: *Good morning.*

J Dane: *Are these meetings always so boring?*

P Daniels: *Wouldn't you have to be paying attention to know they were boring?*

I smirked.

J Dane: *Good point*

P Daniels: *What are you doing here?*

J Dane: *It was on my calendar. You ought to check yours, by the by.*

P Daniels: *I saw it.*

I blinked at my screen and then glanced over to see her adjusting her screen nervously. The girl from finance sat down, and when Judy began to speak again, I dived back into my mission.

J Dane: *And what do you think?*

P Daniels: *People can see my computer, you know.*

J Dane: *And seeing what I have to say to you would be the most exciting thing that's happened to any of them all week.*

P Daniels: *Are you always so cocky?*

J Dane: *Yes. Are you always going to avoid my questions?*

I glanced over and caught sight of a pretty pink blush spreading over her cheeks.

P Daniels: *This isn't the time or place.*

J Dane: *I like that blush. It reminds me of the way you look after I've finished fucking you.*

I shot a surreptitious glance her way and nearly grinned as she fumbled frantically at her keyboard.

P Daniels signed off.

I cleared my throat to choke back my chuckle, and Judy looked over at me, startled.

"Mr. Dane?" she asked.

"I'm so sorry to interrupt, but I was wondering if I might borrow my assistant? Something very important has just come up."

"Always." Judy nodded, and I gave Piper a significant look

as I rose from my seat.

"You're sure this can't wait?" Piper asked pointedly, but I gave her a single shake of the head. "I hate to waste everyone's time."

"It can't."

Without so much as another glance in her direction, I stepped from the room and led the way to my office, holding my door open and motioning for her to step inside.

When she followed, I clicked the door closed behind us and drew the blinds to ensure nobody would be able to see what happened next—and I had a few ideas of how I was hoping it might go.

"What do you think you're doing?" she demanded.

"I think I've made myself clear," I shot back, already feeling better just being close to her than I had all weekend. "You had the weekend to decide, and now I want an answer."

"So you decided to crash my meeting?" She shook her head. "You're incredible."

"But you like it. So tell me, what's it going to be?"

"I should say no." She crossed her arms over her chest and narrowed her eyes.

"You should, which means you don't want to."

She was silent for a long moment, her gaze trained on the floor, but then she met my eyes again. "Look, I'm not going to deny there's something here. Some...chemistry or something."

"Good start." I shrugged.

"And I enjoy being with you in a physical way." Her pink cheeks burned brightly, but rather than commenting, I smiled at her, encouraging her to continue.

"So, I'm interested in continuing our...arrangement. On one condition."

"And what's that?" I asked, a fresh wave of triumph sweeping over me.

"I want to be monogamous."

"You what?" I blinked.

In all the affairs I'd had, of course women had asked me this before, but I had always out-and-out refused. For a man like me—with so many business trips and so little time for enjoyment—I'd never liked the idea of limiting my options.

"You heard me. While we're in our arrangement, I don't want you sleeping with other women." Her chest heaved, and her lively eyes were snapping fire.

"Look, if this is about safety, I always wear a condom. I don't see what the problem here is. We had a good time, and—"

"I don't want to be screwing you and sending flowers to other women. It's awkward and weird," she shot back.

"I thought we agreed on this being casual," I cautioned.

"We did." She nodded. "But I want to only be with each other. The same would go for me, of course."

"And if I say no?" I challenged.

"Then the deal is off. I'll see other people. You'll see other people."

I considered this. The idea of watching her come and go in front of my desk, some random man picking her up and taking her out. Some other man inside her...

"What if you were monogamous and—"

She cut me off with a laugh. "Ha! Nope. Both of us or nothing."

I clenched my fist but gave her a solemn single nod.

"Fine, then. We have a deal. But if you check your calendar, I think you'll also find we both have an appointment to keep, and I don't like to be kept waiting."

It was out of character. Totally nuts, whatever this thing we were doing was.

But fuck, I couldn't wait to start.

CHAPTER ELEVEN

PIPER

"You don't think someone will notice us leaving together?" I asked hesitantly.

Of course, I knew by now that not only had this thought never occurred to him, but even if it had, it wouldn't have made the slightest difference in his plans. Around here, he had rule of the roost, and if he wanted to sleep with his assistant, there was nothing anyone or anything could do to stop him.

I, on the other hand, didn't exactly feel like walking past the herds of whispering secretaries every day on my lunch break, and I certainly didn't need anyone thinking I kept my job because I was sleeping with the boss.

Maybe he was the ruler of everything around here, but when it came to this arrangement?

He was going to play by my rules.

As I stared at his Greek God face, I found myself wavering.

Okay, so I was going to *try* to get him to play by my rules.

"And if they do?" he asked, his eyebrows raised.

"Look, you said we weren't going to do this on business time."

"We're not. Your lunch hour is yours to do with as you

please. Unless, of course, you'd rather not." His luscious mouth tipped up in a mocking grin.

He knew my answer as well as I did. I wanted to go. Wanted *him*. Even if it was the worst idea in the world.

And now, with his mahogany desk between us serving as a vivid reminder of all the ways he could work my body into throes of ecstasy...

"Fine," I found myself saying, despite my reservations. "I'll leave for my lunch break," I said, lowering my voice. "In ten minutes, you can leave too and then meet me in the bar at the hotel."

"Are you always going to be so clandestine about this?" he teased. "Should I call you by another name when I see you?"

Ignoring that, I said, "See you there."

Then, turning on my heel, I made for his door, but not before he added, "When I see you there, you'd better not be wearing panties under that skirt."

An ache of need rose between my thighs and I gave him a brief nod before striding past my desk and practically sprinting into the elevator.

Suddenly I felt like a runner racing toward the finish line, and as people shuffled in and out of the elevator car with me, I barely noticed them. All I could think was how I was going to find the nearest bathroom to slide off my tiny black thong... and what he was going to do when he found out I'd followed his instructions.

In a flash of memory, I thought of the way he'd used my skirt as an anchor, pulling himself deeper and deeper into me. Maybe he'd do that again?

But no. Jackson didn't seem like the sort of man who followed a routine. So far, he'd blown my mind on so many levels, my head was spinning.

The elevator dinged, and I realized I'd finally reached the ground level of the office building. Trying to act natural, I squared my shoulders and rushed toward the revolving glass doors, my heels clicking on the marble floor.

Logically, I knew nobody knew what was happening—that nobody would even blink an eye when they saw Jackson down here ten minutes from now—but somehow it all still felt illicit. Like their eyes followed me, knowing what I was about to do.

But even with the weight of all those imaginary eyes on me, I couldn't bring myself to feel ashamed or embarrassed. Instead, I felt...well, sexy. Empowered. I held my head a little higher, imagining Jackson as he walked across the hotel lobby toward me, that hunger in his eyes.

All for me.

It was crazy. Nuts, really. Completely out of character, yet somehow it felt so right.

Luckily, the walk to the hotel was a short one—it was just around the corner, so close that it was likely a happy hour favorite for the people who worked in the business district. As I walked into the lobby, though, it was clear that it wasn't a favorite lunch spot. The hotel bar was nearly empty save a few older gentlemen sipping amber liquid from highball glasses on the edge of the bar. Briefly I debated heading over but instead settled into a booth in the far corner of the room.

Jackson wasn't even here yet, but my heart was already racing. At this rate, I was going to drop dead of anticipation before he walked in. I was just about to head to the ladies' room to take off my underwear and pat my hot cheeks with cool water when, too soon, I spotted him. He was striding toward me, his hands tucked lazily in his pockets, his dark hair falling slightly over his eyes.

I stared at him, shaking my head in rueful disbelief. He hadn't waited the ten minutes. In fact, it seemed like he hadn't even waited two. But then, how could I have ever expected him to do something that was completely and totally his idea?

I should've been irritated. Instead, another sizzle shot through me. He was a man who marched to his own beat. Did what he wanted and took charge. The feminist in me should be totally turned off, but instead, my knees started to shake with excitement.

This guy was turning me into some sort of sexual deviant, and I had to admit, I kind of liked it.

Wordlessly, he slid into the booth beside me and then dropped one warm palm on my naked knee, searing me with the heat of his skin. The waiter approached, and Jackson ordered for us—two glasses of Cabernet. He waited until the other man's back was turned before leaning in close to me.

"Did you follow my instructions?" he asked, though before I could reply, his fingers were snaking up the inside of my thigh, gently spreading my legs apart until he felt the rough lace of my thong.

"Oh, Piper," he murmured, shaking his head in mock disappointment.

"You didn't exactly give me time," I hissed. "What happened to waiting ten minutes?"

"I wanted to, but then I saw your ass in that skirt while you were getting on the elevator and...well, a man has needs." He offered me his wolf's grin, and I narrowed my eyes.

"Well, now you have to pay the price. I'm still wearing my panties, and you're just going to have to live with it."

He looked about ready to answer, but then the waiter reappeared with our beverages.

"Thanks so much. And we're only here for the one, so we'll take the check," Jackson said with a smile.

The waiter disappeared, and so did Jackson's smile. His heated gaze locked on to my mouth, and I could feel my nipples tighten beneath my blouse.

"Now, where were we?" he asked silkily. "Ah, I remember now. We were talking about punishment."

"Exactly," I said, pausing to gulp down a swallow of wine to soothe my dry throat. "The underwear is your punishment for not waiting—"

"Nope. I mean *your* punishment. For not doing as I asked."

"Ridiculous," I murmured, but I could already feel my body responding to the threat that felt way more like a promise.

"It's an option. That's all I'm saying," he said with a casual shrug that belied the tension in his muscles. Dear Lord, was this man sexy. Like a tiger, all sleek, hard muscle and barely restrained power.

"And the other option?" I pressed, my voice breathy and thin.

"I could make do with what we have." He traced a line back up to the hem of my panties, pushed them aside, and rolled a finger over the seam of my sex. "If I choose to."

I shivered, and another rush of need took hold of me as his finger pushed deeper, teasing me. I shot a panicked glance around the room, but there was no one looking our way. And even if they did, the way he was angled in front of me probably made it look to an outsider like he was whispering something in my ear.

"What do you think I should do?" he asked.

"I-I don't think you should stop," I whispered as he nipped my earlobe sharply with the edge of his teeth. I gasped and could feel his smile against my skin.

"I think I will. And let it be a lesson to you." He pulled away, and my breath caught again, my knees shaking as he righted my skirt. He settled across from me again, leaving me staring at him.

"I..." I started, but I didn't know what to say. Instead, my gaze searched his as he reached for his glass of wine and clinked it against my own.

"To a deal well struck."

"Sure. To that," I muttered, wondering yet again if a person could literally die of need.

Because if so? Somebody was going to need to call the coroner. Stat.

He smirked again, eyeing me over the top of his glass while he took a sip.

"What's so funny?" I demanded, taking my own glass with a shaking hand.

"You," he said simply. "You're trying to be cool and collected when I know what you really want."

"And what is it that I want?"

"Honestly?" He ran a hand over his square jaw as he let his gaze trail over me again. "Well, first of all, you want me to hide underneath this tablecloth and lick you until you make a scene."

I squeezed my thighs together to quell the surge of need that rose in me at the very thought.

"And then?"

"Then you want me to take you up to one of these fancy rooms and fuck you hard and deep until you scream."

That was about right, but hell if I was going to admit it.

I ran my index finger down the front of my blouse and popped the top button open with a flick of my fingers, baring a few inches of creamy skin. Jackson went suddenly quiet, his gaze locked on my hand.

"Thing is, boss man...you want that too, don't you?"

I popped another button, feeling like a fucking Amazon warrior high with power.

"So we can sit here talking all day, or we can go upstairs and do what we've both been wanting to do since we walked in. Your call."

I managed to take another sip of wine without spilling a drop, despite my trembling hands.

"What's it gonna be?" I asked, eyeing him like he was my last meal on death row.

"I'm going to pay the check," he managed through gritted teeth. He nodded toward the approaching waiter. Quickly glancing at the bill, he dropped some money into the leather billfold and then turned his attention back to me.

"Enjoying your drink?" he asked.

"I can barely taste it," I answered honestly. All I could think about was how his lips would taste on mine. What he was going to do to me when we were finally alone. How he would satisfy the needy ache between my thighs.

"Well, if you don't think you can enjoy the rest, it's better that we don't waste our time. What do you think?"

Swallowing hard, I nodded and then allowed him to take my hand and lead me across the room and back into the hotel lobby.

Rather than stopping for a room key, though, he led me into the elevators.

I frowned. "What are we doing?" I asked.

"You said this was supposed to happen on your lunch hour. So I'm giving you a choice." The elevator swung into action, but just as quickly he pressed the emergency stop. "I happen to know that the video cameras in these elevators don't work."

My breath caught in my throat. "So what's my choice?" I forced myself to ask.

His smile widened. "Whether you want to grip one of the handles or get on your knees."

He lifted an eyebrow, eyes blazing, looking every bit like the devil himself out to make a deal.

I was sure he'd made the offer just for the shock value, to make me squirm and blush. But he'd freed a whole new side of me, and I wasn't about to pass up an opportunity like this.

"Why not have both?" I replied.

Then, taking another step toward him, I sank to my knees and unzipped his fly while he unbuckled his belt with a groan of approval. My hands were still shaking, but as he lowered his pants and boxers and his thick, hard length sprang out, I wetted my lips.

He was perfection. Long and thick and straight. I'd never felt more sexy, more free. And I was determined to show him exactly how much that meant to me.

I bent low and pulled his throbbing cock into my mouth, my heart hammering.

How was I going to go back to the way my life was before? How was I going to give this—give *him*—up?

His fingers slid into my hair, and those thoughts melted away under the heat that sizzled between us.

This wasn't a time to worry. It was a time to live and embrace this window of pure joy. And I wasn't going to waste a second of it.

CHAPTER TWELVE

JACKSON

Hardly anyone came into the office on Saturday.

It was always an option, of course—including overtime pay. But on a sunny May afternoon like this? I could hardly expect to find people sitting in their gray cubicles, staring at their computer screens and clacking away on their keyboards.

In fact, if it hadn't been for the upcoming merger, I might have been out on the town too, enjoying the sunshine... or, better yet, watching it pour in through Piper's bedroom window. If there was a window in her bedroom.

Over the past week, our arrangement had been working well. We met during lunch breaks or after work, but I'd never been over to her place, and I was starting to get curious. I knew that she walked to work, so she couldn't have lived too far off, but that was as much as I knew. And, if I was being honest with myself, as much as I knew about her.

From the three times we'd been together since Monday in the elevator, I was learning how to make her back arch into me and how to get her cheeks to turn that pretty rosy color I loved. But other than her hyper-organization and the few items on her schedule I was able to view?

Piper Daniels was as much a mystery to me as the pyramids.

And for some strange reason, it was beginning to piss me off.

Tapping my fingers along the edge of my desk, I picked up the receiver, dialed the number I'd already memorized, and waited as it rang, and rang, and rang again. There was a click followed by a cool, robotic voice instructing me to leave a message.

Frowning, I hung up.

Where would Piper be on a Saturday morning in a city full of people she didn't know? And why the fuck hadn't she brought her cell phone? Or was she just screening my calls? The thought made me frown.

It was too early to go to a bar or a club. Maybe out for brunch? Or a run in the park? Did she like to sit on the edge of the pond and look at fish? Or maybe the library?

Did she even like to read?

Letting out a snarl of frustration, I dialed her number again and waited as it went to voice mail again. Apparently, wherever she was, she was too busy to take my call.

Unless she was at home and sleeping in...

If that was the case, then I knew exactly what to do.

It only took me five minutes to pull up her employee information form. I quickly entered her address into my phone and started the route there. After stashing the few bits and pieces I'd been working on, I headed out to the parking garage to my car, cursing myself the whole way.

This was ridiculous. She wasn't some southern belle I was

wooing to become my bride or something. But now that it was lodged in my mind...the thought of bringing her breakfast in bed and climbing in beside her?

I couldn't shake it.

When I finally got onto the street, I made a pit stop at the little bakery at the corner and got a dozen assorted pastries before following the route again. It was no wonder she walked to work. Her place wasn't far off, though the neighborhood was hardly one I'd ever visited in my free time. It was filled with apartments and little shops, but if you didn't call the place home, you'd have no reason to visit here.

She was new to the city, I knew that much, but I'd never thought to ask where she'd come from. Or why she'd come here at all.

Totally the norm for me, but I realized now with a start how strange it was and how much I suddenly wanted to know the answers to those unasked questions.

When I reached the squat, brick building, I passed a man in a uniform leaning against the entryway pillars and smoking something that did not smell like a cigarette. Nodding to him, I stepped into the building and glanced around for a place to have her ring me up. Only there wasn't one. Instead, there was just a set of elevators and two stairwell doors flanking an empty mailroom and desk. Blinking, I let myself into the elevator and leaned back against the rail.

Was this how she lived? Anyone could just roll up to her apartment door. There was no security of any kind.

I didn't like that one fucking bit.

The doors dinged, and I stepped into a hallway that

smelled just like the guy out front. I glanced both ways until I saw the door marked number eight at the end of the hall.

Holding the white bakery box in one hand, I knocked and then waited for the sound of footsteps. It wasn't until I heard them that I realized I'd been holding my breath.

The footsteps slowed to a stop in front of the door, and without a pause, the door swung open to reveal Piper with a towel on her head, blinking up at me in shock.

"Hey. Uh, what are you doing here?" she asked, raising a hand to her towel as her cheeks turned pink.

"I should ask you the same thing. This place is a fucking death trap."

"Excuse me?" Her eyes—one lined with makeup and one without—narrowed.

"I just walked up here, and you didn't even check to see who it was before swinging the door open. I bet it wasn't even locked. And what the fuck with no buzzer or anything?"

"I'm sorry, is this some employee safety inspection I wasn't aware of?" She crossed her arms over her chest and glared at me.

She looked cute as fuck in her towel turban and bare toes, but I wasn't going to let that sway me. This was serious.

"Look, I know you're a sweet and trusting soul, but this isn't whatever backcountry town you came from. You have to watch yourself."

"You mean Chicago?" she shot back.

I paused. Okay, so maybe not backcountry, but that only pissed me off more. She should know better. "That doesn't change my point. There is literally no security here."

"There's a doorman," she said. "He was probably just outside smoking."

"Well, someone needs to fire him, then, or get him to do his job."

She rolled her eyes and stepped back with an impatient wave of her hand. "Did you want to come in, or was your plan to stand on my doorstep and yell at me?"

I took a step inside and offered her the box of pastries. "I got one of everything. Wasn't sure what your favorite was."

"Cheese Danish," she said, taking the box and carrying it over to the island on the far side of the room.

The place was a loft so small I wondered for a moment what exactly I was paying her, but then she interrupted my thoughts. "What brings you here on your Saturday with no call and no warning?"

"I called twice," I said.

She popped open the box, and her eyes lit up as she scanned its contents.

"And when I didn't answer you figured you'd come over and...what? Ransack the place?" she chirped, suddenly seeming more cheerful than a few seconds before.

Okay, so apparently showing up bearing baked goods had earned me some brownie points, even though she was mad. I made a quick mental note.

Buy lots of Danish.

She selected a treat from the box and took a monster-sized bite. I followed her lead, taking a chocolate croissant from the box and examining it.

"I thought you might like to see the city. It's a beautiful

day, and you're new around here, so I thought..."

She grinned. "You're getting soft, boss. I kind of like it."

She licked a fleck of glaze from her bottom lip, and I resisted the urge to show her exactly how soft I wasn't. I'd been irritated all morning because I wanted to get to know her a little better. Lying in bed all day, as awesome as that might be, wasn't going to scratch this particular itch.

"Anyway," I pressed on. "You're only trying to distract me from the fact that you live in the gateway to hell. This neighborhood isn't safe. You should let me find you a place in one of the buildings I own. Something with cameras and 24-hour security. And buzzers."

"It'd be nice to have packages delivered someplace they wouldn't get stolen," she acknowledged, glancing around with a satisfied grin. "But to be honest, I sort of like this place. It has character."

I surveyed the old wooden framework around her windows and scrubbed a hand over my jaw in irritation. "That's one word for it."

"I'm not talking any more about this. I want to hear all about your big plans for today." She took another bite of her Danish. "Where are you taking me?"

I sure as shit wasn't just going to drop it, but I wasn't going to let it ruin our day, either.

I tucked it away to chew on later that night and turned my attention away from the dingy windows back to her.

"I don't really have any, exactly. I don't really know what you like to do." I glanced around her apartment again, looking for some sign or hint of where to start. There was no video game system, and while there were a few paintings hanging on the walls, the place was mostly covered in family photos. I walked toward one of them and pressed my finger to the glass as I examined a girl who looked almost exactly like Piper.

"Who is this?" I asked.

"My sister," she said. "She's the one who set up the, uh, dating profile."

"Right," I laughed. "So, tell me, what do you want to learn about our fine city?"

"How to get Hamilton tickets?" she asked cheekily, eyebrows raised.

"Try again," I said dryly. "I'm pretty spectacular, but I'm not magic."

"How about we hit the streets and just see what we see, huh?"

"You? Miss organization and plan-every-second-of-the-day-out wants to wing it?" I considered for a moment and then gave her a solemn nod. "Okay."

I was careful to make sure she locked all her doors and windows before we started on our journey. As we passed the doorman, he was still leaning against the wall outside. Piper grinned at him.

"Hey, Lou."

"'Sup, Pipes?" he asked as she kept going, not noticing—or, more likely, choosing to ignore—my grimace of displeasure.

"He's not going to do his job if you act like what he's doing is okay," I said.

"Lucky for me and him both, I'm not his boss." She winked. "Now come on. Did you come to fight with me all day or to show me around the city?"

"A little hard to show you around the city when I don't know where to start."

"How about with your favorite place?" she offered.

I thought about it and then nodded.

"Yeah, okay. Come with me." And without even thinking about it, I grabbed her hand and led her off into the heart of the city, feeling better than I could remember feeling in months.

CHAPTER THIRTEEN

PIPER

I wasn't sure what to expect. Maybe that he'd whisk me away to some underground jazz club or to his favorite tailored suit shop. Maybe just to some hole-in-the-wall burger joint that nobody had ever heard of. With a guy like Jackson, I could never be sure.

But, as we sailed down the avenue, I had a few guesses.

"The M&M store in Times Square?" I asked, grinning at him.

"Nope," he said, squeezing my hand.

"What about, um, the Ferris wheel in the Toys 'R' Us?"

"Not there either," he said.

"I'm running out of guesses," I complained.

"Good news for me."

"Hey!" I popped him lightly on the shoulder, but he pressed on, turning the corner and trying to hide his ever-widening grin.

"So no place touristy?" I asked.

"I didn't say that either."

"You haven't said much of anything. At all."

It was true—from the moment we'd left my apartment,

he'd barely uttered more than a few words, though most had been in answer to my never-ending questions about where exactly he was taking me. But as much as I was peppering him with constant questions, I was walking on air.

He'd come to my apartment building, and not only was he concerned for my safety, he'd whisked me off on a date.

A real, relationship-style date, complete with the breakfast of champions and handholding. My heart felt like it was going to explode. I hadn't had this kind of male attention in a long while, and while screaming orgasms were nice, I had missed this casual comradery more than I had been aware.

"I want it to be a surprise."

We turned a corner and walked past booths of street vendors selling pottery and scarves. Jackson barely looked at them, but I paused, my eyes wide, and inspected the cute creations.

"Come on," he said.

"Fine, fine, I'm coming."

In front of us stretched the vast, wide steps of the Museum of Modern Art, though the street in front of it was flanked by vendors and lines of tourists.

"We're here."

"What do you mean?" I looked around. "The food trucks? We're going to wait in this line for an hour." The food did smell delicious, but I'd just scarfed down a plate-sized Danish and was hardly ready for lunch yet.

He shook his head and then gestured to the huge, pillared museum. "You told me to take you to my favorite place in the city. Here it is."

"The Art Museum?" I blinked at the building and the flood of families coming and going through the wide-open doors. Of all the places I'd expected him to choose, this wasn't even on the list.

Keeping me on my toes, aren't you, Jackson?

He considered me for a minute and then said, "Let's go inside."

Placing his hand on the small of my back, he led me up the wide marble steps until we reached the atrium. On a sunny Saturday like this, it felt like almost every person in the city was trying to get inside the place, and we waited as the queue in front of us thinned and people took up their walking-tour headphones and joined still more groups. To the side, a bunch of kids were assembling for what looked like a church field trip, and I grinned as one of the little boys lightly pulled a girl's pigtails.

I almost pointed them out to Jackson, but then his hand found mine and he was giving me a small blue button to pin to my shirt.

"Thanks," I murmured and affixed the little circle to my clothes before stepping into the first room.

I had to admit, it was a good showing from Jackson. For the next ten minutes, I strolled around the room in awe, marveling at the paintings and sculptures.

"So this is your favorite place in the city," I said again, and Jackson gave me a solemn nod.

"What's your favorite part?"

"There are so many." He shrugged. "The exhibits change all the time, and then there's the exhibit with the old sixties and seventies furniture that looks impossible as a functional piece in someone's house. There was an Andy Warhol exhibit I liked here once."

"Andy Warhol? Really?" I raised my eyebrows.

He nodded.

"Affinity for Campbell's soup?"

"Just the tomato," he shot back.

Taking my hand again, he led me toward the newer exhibits, expertly weaving through each of the rooms like he really had been here many, many times before. He knew the place by heart.

Finally, we reached a room filled with huge canvases with swathes of colors. Some faded from one color to another while others were blocks of colors that seemed to exist independent of the rest of the canvas. They were so simple, but the simplicity in and of itself was oddly intriguing, and I found myself moving a little closer, taking in the brushstrokes and the sheer craftsmanship.

"A favorite of yours?" I asked.

"Rothko. He's a classic."

I nodded. "I can see why. His stuff is..."

"Incredible," he filled in, and no part of me wanted to argue. "You like art," he said. It wasn't a question.

"I do. It was my major in college."

"College wasn't on your résumé," he said, his head cocked in my direction.

"No, well...it wouldn't be. Didn't graduate." I shrugged.

"Why not?" he asked.

I glanced at him from over my shoulder, lifting one

eyebrow. "I'll show you mine if you show me yours. Why won't you tell me for real why you love this place so much?"

I was going on pure instinct, but something told me there was more to his affinity for art than he was letting on.

He hedged again and then glanced around, almost as if he was making sure nobody could overhear us. "I used to come here a lot growing up."

I didn't say anything and waited for the rest. With the look he had on his face—full of uncertainty totally at odds with his usual personality—I wasn't about to press him. Not right then, anyway.

"So, uh, I grew up in the system. Not many people know that," he added, his gaze locked on the painting in front of us. "Some houses weren't so bad, but a lot of my foster parents just had me around for the government check. During the day, I was left to my own devices, and more often than not, I found myself here."

My heart squeezed, and I had to fight the desire to close the gap between us and squeeze him until the sadness in his eyes faded away.

"Why here?" I asked softly.

"Because it was free. For school-age kids back then, anyway. I used to look at the paintings and imagine a day when I could have my own house to put up something so beautiful. Or, to be completely honest, to have enough money to spend it on something as frivolous as art. Even if it was a print from a big box store, that was more money than I ever had back then. But, you know, as time went on, I got a little more enterprising. There was an architecture exhibit, and I thought, well, I couldn't paint, but I knew how to use a hammer and nails."

"So you did," I said, fighting a mix of sad tears and a deep, soul-aching pride in him and the man he'd become, despite such terrible odds.

He nodded. "So that's what I did. When I was eighteen, I moved to the shittiest area I could find outside the city and used all my saved money to buy the worst house in town. I flipped it and used the money to buy two more houses. Then four."

"Then you built an empire."

He grinned. "Empire is one way of putting it."

"I didn't know. They should put you in some sort of magazine. You could inspire kids like you."

His face darkened. "It's not exactly something I like to talk about. Those are the highlights, but growing up in the foster care system, at least back then, isn't something I care to think about or relive. Your turn now."

I wanted to ask him why, to understand the ripple of pain that passed over his expression, but the tone of his voice was clear—the time for discussion was over. Now it was my turn to spill.

"I didn't go to college right away. When I got out of high school, I traveled around to find myself."

"Ah, one of those girls." He shoved his hands in his pockets.

"Yep, that's me." I rolled my eyes. "Anyway, when I got home, I decided the place for me to go was school. It was always something that had mattered to me. I was a straight-A student—"

"I had no doubt," he said.

"And I had a knack for learning, so I threw myself in. Then, you know, I met this guy, and he wanted to run away with me, so I dropped out and he...dropped me." Shame bubbled beneath the surface, and I tried to push it aside. "I still decided to run away. Just, this time, it was by myself."

"And that's how you ended up here," he concluded.

"That's it in a nutshell." I nodded.

"Could have been worse," he said, and though I knew this was his way of trying to soothe me, I couldn't help but poke at his logic.

"How's that?" I asked.

"Well, you could have married him or had his baby and then had him walk away. That would've been worse."

"I guess so, yeah." I shrugged.

"Or worse, you could have never met me." The mischievous glint returned to his eyes, and I gave him a playful punch on the arm before taking his hand in mine again. I let out a breath, relieved to have things on a lighter note but also somehow soothed that we'd shared some of our darkest times with one another. I finally was starting to feel like I was seeing the whole man instead of just one piece of him. And I liked it.

A lot.

"Come on, Mr. Modesty. Show me your other favorites. I'm interested now."

Next, he took me to another room filled with paintings of single words like *love*, *honesty*, and *respect*. He studied each of them closely, mentioning the font and pointing out the brush strokes. In the next room, he showed me things he'd noticed about oil painting, explained the difference between the mediums, and then took me to the room full of old sixties' vacuum cleaners and wildly shaped coffee tables.

"I can see why you'd find this place inspiring. I want to write the great American novel just walking around this place," I said.

"Me too. Bad news is that I'm a terrible writer." He took me by the crook of the arm and led me back out to the vendors outside, stopping to grab me a cupcake from one of them before we leaned back on the steps and watched the hordes of people coming and going.

"Do you mind if I ask you something?" I said when I'd finished my cupcake that I hadn't even realized I was hungry for.

"What's that?" he asked.

"If you had such a terrible time in the system, why did you stay in New York?"

"Would you believe me if I told you it was because this is the center of the world and I needed to be part of it?"

"Not for a second," I shot back.

"You know me well," he laughed. "I'll warn you, though, it's not a happy ending."

"Don't you end up meeting me?"

He rolled his eyes. "I was dating a girl who went to Columbia, and she got pregnant. I moved back here to be with her and the baby, and I bought an apartment building so she could keep going to school."

"Oh," I said, my mind spinning.

"She was nice enough, but she miscarried in the third month, and then we decided it wasn't worth staying together if we'd only been doing it for the baby."

"That's devastating. You must have been heartbroken."

"Yes and no." He pursed his lips and then looked me deep in the eyes. "Would you think I was a bad person if I told you that I was sad for her but a tiny part of me was relieved? Not that I would've ever wished for it, but I didn't love that girl and I don't want children. I did it because it was the right thing to do, of course. But ever since then, I've been careful to make sure there was never a repeat."

"You're not a bad person," I said, but my heart gave a little squeeze.

"Thanks. I guess if you've lived through everything I have—if you saw the pressures and the stresses of people trying to raise children—it's just not for me."

I took a deep breath. "I can understand that."

We spent the rest of the day roaming the city, and as much as I loved his company, a little part of the joy inside me had faded. Both at the thought of a young Jackson, alone and confused and unloved—and at the realization that he didn't want kids.

I shouldn't have minded. Hell, this one date was more than I'd ever expected from him, but I couldn't help it. There was a part of me that felt a little heartsick at the thought.

Later that evening, we walked back to my apartment, and all the while he lectured me on the importance of locking my door and making sure I knew what was happening in my neighborhood. In truth, though, I was only half listening. A part of me was still back on the steps of the museum, thinking over everything he'd said and trying to understand the reason

I'd been so affected.

It hit me right as we walked through the door of my building, and it was like a slap.

I was falling for him. *Wrong.* I had already fallen. *Hard.* Quirks and stern lips and all, I was head over heels.

Which, when it came to Jackson, was way, way too deep.

CHAPTER FOURTEEN

JACKSON

Monday came in like a sledgehammer, taking out all my well-laid plans and sending everything into freefall.

I'd just hung up the phone with my legal department, and apparently the merger we'd spent months prepping for was at risk. There was some sort of zoning issue that might hold up a lucrative build, and the company on the other side of the merger was getting cold feet. All through the morning, before any of my regular employees walked through the doors, I was on the phone with managers at the other company, and then merger specialists, and still more acclaimed consultants, until my throat was dry.

To be honest, when the lights of the day went up and people started shuffling through the door, I barely even noticed. Instead, I was focused on the constant steady beat of my heart and the icy dread slowly seeping into my veins.

Of course, I wasn't worried about myself. Hell, I wasn't even worried about the company. Ninety percent of mergers didn't go through, and that was a possibility I'd considered when I'd started this venture. But that didn't change the fact that even here, on the executive level, some of my employees would be losing their jobs if I couldn't make this work.

Vaguely, I thought of Clara in HR. She'd spent the last two weeks circling the office to get pledges for her son's Jump Rope for Heart Disease event. Her husband had died of a heart attack only last year, and it meant everything to her that her little boy was taking action so young.

Then there was Frank. He'd asked for a raise a few weeks ago and for good reason. He'd been with the company almost since its inception, and he was helping to send his grandchildren to college.

The list went on. Every single one of these people had a story to tell—a reason they needed this job more than anything else. And the way I ran my company? There was no fat to trim. Anyone we lost here would be essential, and it would be impossible for me to reckon with the idea of letting them go.

So I wouldn't.

I just had to figure out how to avoid it.

Clicking on an email labeled Urgent—as if everything else wasn't—I glanced at my computer screen as a gentle knock sounded on my doorframe.

I swiveled in my chair to catch sight of Piper standing tall and patient with my first cup of coffee in her hand.

"You're here early," she said. "Half the office still isn't here."

"Got a call last night. Had to come in for some meetings."

Her brow furrowed. "Is everything all right?"

I considered her for a long moment, wondering if I should tell her. It wasn't usually done. Things like this tended to be *need to know* because they caused widespread employee panic over something that might not be a problem after all. Still, she wasn't some gossipy assistant. She was Piper. And somehow I knew she'd have my back.

On a snap judgment, I decided to come clean. "There are issues with the merger that could lead to...downsizing if I don't figure out what to do."

"Downsizing?" she repeated and then snapped the office door shut behind her as she made her way to my desk and set down my cup of coffee.

I nodded. "I'm not sure on what scale yet. It could be very minor."

"I understand. And I don't blame you at all. I'm new and—"

Suddenly realizing how she must have taken my words, I rushed to correct myself. "No, I need an executive assistant. You wouldn't be the one to go."

"That's not fair," she said. "These people have put in more time than me. Any one of them could be a fine assistant."

"That's not the job they'd want."

"You won't know until you ask them," she shot back. "It's only fair. Like I said, I don't want any special treatment."

She made her way to the coffee pot in the corner of the room and began to fix herself a cup, and I was taken aback for a moment as a snatch of a light-blue button caught my eye.

"Are you still wearing your pin from the museum?" I asked.

She shot me a smile over her shoulder. "I thought...well, I thought it would be a nice reminder. But anyway, we have more important things to talk about than that. How are we going to save these jobs?"

"We?" I raised my eyebrows.

"Yes, we. I haven't lost my job yet. I'm your assistant. Let me assist. Tell me, what's our biggest concern? Shareholder confidence?"

I nodded. "There was a massive lead abatement issue with the other company last year. They own most of the buildings in the historic district, so we're trying to corner that market and create refinished, refined luxury apartments with a hint of old-world elegance."

"That's a mouthful." Piper grabbed her fresh cup of coffee and blew on the top of it.

"That's what I said, too. A consultant came up with it, not me."

"Oh, I know you didn't write something that frilly. I've read your memos." She grinned at me from the top of her coffee mug, and for a moment, I allowed myself to imagine how relaxing it would be to ignore the world and fall into Piper for an hour or two. To close the blinds and let all my problems fall away while our bodies eased the tension.

"Lunch today?" I asked.

She shook her head. "We're going to be busy on this. We need all the time we can get. I'll order lunch in for us. Now come on, let's brainstorm."

I nodded my acceptance. Guess it was time to stop thinking with my dick.

"Be right back," she said and then hustled to her desk and reappeared with another huge dry-erase board.

"I'm half convinced you can conjure those from thin air,"

I said.

"If only. Now let's think."

We drew the blinds to keep the other employees from seeing exactly what we were working on, but by the time lunch came around, we had a massive brainstorming board filled with presentation ideas and methods for preventative abatement, innovative strategies for keeping renovation of the apartments in-house, and a plan for not only keeping the jobs we had but creating new ones as well.

Piper wiped her hands together, stepped back, and admired her handiwork.

"Now," she said, "I am going to grab our food so we can figure out how to implement each and every one of these ideas. You start drafting emails. The burger place on the corner sound good?"

I nodded, and she tossed me a glance over her shoulder as she stepped from the room again, leaving me to stare at the massive amount of work and ideas I would never have accomplished on my own.

But then again, that was the magic of Piper. No matter what happened, she seemed to sweep in and magically fix it. Already I could feel the steady, thrumming beat of my heart slowing and relaxing, my shoulders falling back into place where they belonged.

We had come up with a massive plan of attack, but if we were right—and if we devoted ourselves to the work—it just might save jobs.

Who knew? Maybe we'd be successful enough for me to give her a raise and convince her to move from her hole of an apartment.

I smiled to myself. Then I opened my emails and got to work, planning and typing so fast I hardly noticed when Piper reappeared and dropped a burger and fries on my desk before disappearing through the doors again. As the door clicked closed behind her, I let out a little groan of discontent. I liked having her nearby. I liked being able to bounce my ideas off her, but I knew why she wouldn't stay.

She would never allow the other employees to see her with me behind closed doors for too long—no matter the reason. It jeopardized her reputation and mine, and by working at her desk she was safeguarding her status as a professional.

I understood that.

But that didn't change the fact that I wanted her here.

The day wore on, and between bites of my now-cold burger, I'd intercepted so many emails and schedules that I hardly had time to start in on our battle plan. When five o'clock came around, my door opened, and I looked up expecting to see Piper with her bag on her shoulder, ready to head out for the day.

"I had the assistants meeting this afternoon so we can make sure we finish this presentation for the shareholders. I don't want another burger. How about salad for dinner?" she asked.

I frowned. "Your work day is over. You don't have to—"

"I don't have to do anything, but I'm asking you, salad or something else? Maybe tacos? Sandwiches?"

"I'm not hungry."

"Salad, then. I'll put them in the fridge until we're ready

to eat."

Without another word, she headed out the door again. I smiled to myself as I stared at the wide brainstorming map in front of me and selected the first task.

For the next three days, things pressed on the same way. In the mornings, Piper and I would review where we were in terms of our battle plan, and business as usual would creep in and get in the way. She ordered us lunch and dinner and stayed until all the lights went out in the building. When they did, she would walk into my office, sit on my couch, and work there with me, shooting ideas back and forth and taking notes on what needed to be done next.

Only then would we relieve our mutual tension in the best way I knew how.

It was a perfect, elegant system, but the long hours were beginning to wear on both of us. Already, dark, puffy circles were slowly forming under Piper's eyes, and more often than not, I would get an email in the middle of the night explaining in some detail what needed to be done the next day, which let me know she was taking the work home with her just as I was.

On the fourth day, after everyone had gone home, I turned to her and asked her point-blank. "Why are you working so hard on this? I appreciate it, but you should go home and get some sleep."

"I'm not having this argument with you," she said, not bothering to look up from her laptop.

"You're not going to lose your job. You really don't—"

"I'm not worried about my job," she snapped, glaring at me. "I'm worried about the company. And"—she glanced away—"you know, you. This is important to you. This place is everything you've worked for. Now stop bothering me, and let's get it done."

I surveyed her for a long moment, a warm feeling spreading through my chest. "Is that really how you feel?"

She nodded, and suddenly my mouth went dry. Jesus, when was the last time someone had cared about me? Truly cared about whether I ate right or took care of myself or felt responsible for my employees to the point that it was causing me sleepless nights?

And now here Piper was, just a hookup, I'd told myself. Just a temporary employee. But she was more than that. So much more.

I dropped the file folder in my hands and closed my fingers around her wrists, overwhelmed by a wave of something I refused to name, as I drew her close to me.

CHAPTER FIFTEEN

PIPER

Jackson's lips pressed over mine, and I was lost. The man was masterful at so many things, but kissing may have been his strongest suit. I parted my lips on a shaky breath, and he used the opportunity to sweep his tongue gently against mine, coaxing a moan to rumble in my chest.

He broke away, his eyes seductive and locked on mine. "You've been working so hard. I hate that the only way I repay you is by orgasms."

I chuckled, placing my palm on the rough stubble of his cheek. "Yes, it's awful."

I loved the way he looked at me—like I had his complete attention. He petted one hand along my hair, admiring me as I stood before him in my stocking feet. I'd kicked off my heels hours ago.

Jackson smiled and pressed a chaste kiss to my lips. "I've never met anyone quite like you, Piper."

I raised my eyebrows—the man was not known for his attempts at sweet sentiment. "Yeah? How so?"

His hands skimmed down my waist and settled on my ass. "You're the total package. Smart, fiery, devoted, and with a nice, tight little pussy."

I chuckled again. There was the Jackson I knew. I was about to point out that he was just rather large, but I decided to let him believe what he wanted to. "I'm glad you think so."

He moved his hands around to the back of my skirt and gave the zipper a little tug. "What do you say? Let me fuck that tight pussy tonight."

As if I would deny him. As if I was even capable of that. Anytime Jackson was near, it was like all the oxygen in the room had been sucked out and replaced with pure, potent pheromones.

I reached for the bulge beneath his trousers and gave him a playful squeeze. "It's awfully late, Mr. Dane. I should probably be getting home."

He shook his head. "And deny me? You wouldn't dare defy a superior would you, Miss Daniels?"

"What did you have in mind?" I asked, my voice growing breathless. His cock was so damned tempting.

Jackson's full lips quirked up in a smile. "How about I let you ride my face until you come and then ride my dick until you can't walk straight?"

I swallowed a trembling sigh. "Sold."

Jackson lifted me from the floor and hauled me to his chest for another smoldering kiss that he didn't break as he carried me over to the small couch in his office. When Jackson set me down gently on the cushion, he didn't join me like I expected. He watched me for a moment with hooded eyes.

"I think our progress tonight calls for a toast. You're not a whiskey girl, are you?"

I was surprised he wasn't diving into the main event but was then struck by the thought that maybe he didn't want to go home alone any more than I did. Was my big, bad, cocky boss prolonging our evening together? Far be it for me to argue.

I smiled. "If the occasion calls for it."

"That's my girl." The rich tone of his voice sent a fresh wave of desire washing over me.

Jackson returned with lowball glasses, each with a measure of amber-colored liquor.

"Cheers." I accepted my glass, clinking it against his. We each took a couple of sips, the vibe turning to a relaxed one as the alcohol eased the tension in my shoulders. Sometime after dinner, Jackson had killed the overhead florescent lights, opting just for the dimly lit lamp on his desk—for which I was immediately grateful.

"I really appreciate you, Piper. Even if you didn't have the world's hottest pussy, I'd still be happy you're my assistant."

I took one more sip of my drink and placed my glass on the table beside his. "I'm happy to hear that."

Jackson's lips quirked up as he watched me rise to my feet.

I unzipped my skirt and let it fall to a puddle at my feet. Slowly, I stripped for him, loving the way his dark eyes heated as he watched me.

Once I was completely nude, Jackson offered his hand. "Come here and let me have a taste."

True to his word, Jackson licked and sucked at my tender flesh until I came with a shout, my body clenching wildly.

And then he guided me to his lap, patiently working all nine inches inside me while letting out sexy, soft groans.

We made love slowly—without any of the teasing or spanking or dirty words I'd come to expect from him.

It was perfect. And as the sweat on our bodies cooled, I was struck by one somber thought—how depressing would it be if this man hadn't come into my life?

CHAPTER SIXTEEN

PIPER

I brushed my fingers over my lips, recalling the gentle pressure of Jackson's kiss from the night before, when my sister's voice over the phone drew me from my reverie.

"Are you even listening to me?" she whined, tapping her finger on the phone. "Hellllooo?"

"I'm here," I said, cheeks flushing at how easily distracted I'd become lately. I gripped the phone more tightly and willed myself to pay attention.

"I was asking you, how is Mr. Hottie?" Hailey sing-songed the last word, and I did my best not to snap at her.

For the past hour, I'd been trying to catch up with her all while trying to skillfully avoid this question, but my sister knew me too well to allow that sort of thing to pass.

Unluckily for her, I wasn't willing to give up the goods quite so easily.

"He's fine. But what about Mom's new hobby? Is Dad going crazy with all the glitter or—?"

"Nope, I'm not doing this with you," Hailey said with that stubborn edge to her voice that made my gut clench. "You're telling me details, or I'll take a flight and introduce myself to him and ask him for the answers you're not willing to give me. Your call, big sis."

I rolled my eyes. *Drama queen.* "I already answered you. Things are fine."

"And you're telling me you're not still worried about everyone in the office finding out you're schtuping the boss?"

"No, I think...I think we've been discreet. At least, I hope we have." A little coil of dread rolled through my stomach at the thought, but I tried to brush it back.

If anyone thought anything about our relationship, they certainly hadn't said anything to me about it. And, of course, it was true that I spent every morning in his office with the blinds drawn, but that was because we were still unraveling the mess that was the merger. Everyone in the office knew what we were doing, even if they didn't know exactly how serious the situation was.

"He's actually been pretty stressed out lately," I said, finding myself caving, if only to have someone to talk to about all of this. Truth was, every day, I was getting in deeper, growing more attached. When the time finally came—and, let's be honest, this was Jackson, so it would—letting go was going to be the hardest thing I'd ever had to do.

"I have an idea of how you can fix that." There was a laugh in Hailey's voice that I tried to ignore.

"Why don't we ever talk about your sex life instead of mine?" I asked.

"Something has to exist for you to talk about it," Hailey answered, apparently nonplussed. "I've been in a serious dry spell. Let me live vicariously through you, sister dear. I want to know more about him. I saw his profile, but it barely said anything. What's his deal? Why do you like him? Is he funny? Do you like him more than just someone to screw around with?"

"Woah, tiger, slow down," I said with a chuckle.

"Sorry. You're just making it really hard to fantasize about how awesome your life is by being so stingy with the deets. Plus, I need to tell Mom something about him."

"Mom?" I choked.

"She's asking me all sorts of questions about him. What's he like?"

"I'll tell you something if you promise not to tell Mom," I shot back immediately.

"Deal." I could practically see Hailey's grin through the phone. No doubt this had been her plan all along—threaten me and then get me to spill once the threat was gone, but I was so relieved to have the specter of our mother off my back, I didn't care. I loved our mom, but she was what people tended to call "a real piece of work," so I tried to keep our visits biannual and our phone calls to once-a-week check-ins if I could help it.

Hailey sighed, and I knew I'd reached the end of the line. I had to give her something here, or she was going to ratchet up from annoying to relentless.

I thought hard, trying to figure out how to explain Jackson to someone who had never met him.

"He's a serious kind of guy," I started.

"I figured that from his picture," Hailey said. "Serious good or serious bad, though?"

"What's the difference?"

Hailey sighed. "Well, isn't it obvious? Serious good is like 'I'd die for the woman I love,' and serious bad is like...cold. Like he's humorless."

I thought of the glint of mischief in Jackson's eyes when he messaged me to meet him around the corner at the hotel.

"Serious good, then," I said.

"Good," Hailey said. "So what else, then?"

"He cares a lot about his company."

"And his family?" Hailey prompted. "Is he a my-mother-is-a-goddess-on-earth sort of guy or a guy who thinks his mother ruined him for life? Or...?"

"None of the above," I answered patiently. "He's on his own. No family."

"Wow. No family. And serious too." Hailey whistled. "Sounds dark and mysterious."

"Sort of, I guess."

"And you like him? As more than just—?"

"Maybe we should talk about something else," I said. "You haven't told me anything about your job. What's going on there?"

"It exists. There's not much more to say about it. I want to know more about Christian Grey over there, though. How is he in bed? Does he have a play room?"

I considered our encounter in the conference room the week before, our time in the elevator, and even the first night on that rooftop garden.

"No, no play room." It was better than that. He didn't have a room full of mysteries, but there was no telling which room he would claim as our own. Now every time I stepped into an elevator, it was with the memory of his lips on my body. Whenever I walked into his office, it was with the knowledge that he'd bent me over his desk and lifted me on top of it more times than I could count.

"Boo," Hailey's voice interrupted my thoughts, and I snapped back to attention. "Well, is he good in bed at least?"

"Hailey, I'm not going to tell you that."

"Because you don't have to. I mean, you guys have been getting it up and down for like a month and a half now. It must be good to keep at it like that."

"A month and a half?"

Had it really been that long? It didn't seem possible. Time was going by so quickly that I—

My heart stopped and then leapt into my throat.

A month and a half. She was right. Our first night together had been right before Cinco de Mayo, and now it was the middle of June. And in all that time...

"Piper? What's wrong?"

"I have to go."

"No way. You sound like someone just shot you in the chest. No fucking around here, tell me what's going on immediately," Hailey demanded, her tone as serious as a heart attack.

I swallowed back another rush of nausea and forced the words through my numb lips.

"I haven't had my period," I whispered, clasping my hand over my mouth before mumbling the rest. "I didn't realize. We've been working so hard, and..."

"Look, it's probably nothing," Hailey rushed. "You've been under a lot of stress at work. Your period always gets wonky when you've got your mind on other things."

"It does," I agreed, though I didn't move my hand from in front of my mouth.

Instead, I was thinking back to that day on the steps of the museum. How Jackson had said he'd always tried to be careful ever since he and his ex had broken up. How he'd said he didn't want the responsibility of raising children.

"The important thing is not to panic," Hailey said, but her voice sounded as if it was coming to me from the end of a long tunnel.

I was long past panic. I just kept thinking of how tired I'd been and how weird my stomach had felt. And how many times Jackson and I had slept together.

Distantly, I heard myself tell her that I'd have to call her back, and then I dashed to the drug store and picked up three pregnancy tests.

The next ten minutes went by in an adrenaline- and fear-induced haze, and before I could even stop shaking, I was back in my apartment bathroom. I wrenched down my pants, more determined to pee than I'd ever been in my entire life.

Carefully, I read the instructions for each test and followed them to the letter, setting timers for every single one and then pacing my apartment as I chewed on my nails—a nasty habit I'd forced myself to break way back in high school.

I couldn't be pregnant. We'd been so careful. Every single time.

If I was, though, everyone in the office would have to find out who the father was. My career would be ruined. And then, of course, there was Jackson himself.

He'd be in the same position he'd been in all those years ago, trapped with a woman who'd only been a casual fling because she was having his baby.

Shit.

I was already starting to freak out.

I didn't know for sure yet and wouldn't for another—I checked my phone—three and a half minutes.

The phone trilled to life, and Hailey's face flashed on the screen. Reluctantly I answered and pressed the phone to my cheek.

"Are you okay?" Hailey asked. "I tried to call you back about seven times. You hung up on me."

"I'm... I don't know," I panted. "I'm dizzy."

I sat on the couch, but the world around me continued to spin.

"Did you go buy a test?" Hailey asked.

"I bought three," I replied.

"Good. That's, uh, prudent. You'll be sure."

"Exactly."

"And then, when it comes out negative, you can move on with your day," my sister said, trying to keep her tone light.

"Exactly. Right." I breathed. A silence stretched between us for a long moment. "But what if I'm pregnant?"

"Well, would you want to... I mean, would you consider—?"

"Adoption?" I asked. "No, I don't think so."

"Or, you know, you have other options too," she said lightly.

I blinked. That hadn't even occurred to me.

"No, I'll keep the baby. If there's a baby to keep. This

might all be nothing."

"It probably is all nothing," Hailey agreed.

I gripped the phone a little tighter and walked carefully back into the bathroom. Against my ear, the phone vibrated, and I knew time was up. This was it. Where the rubber met the road.

"I'm going to check them now," I said, but Hailey said nothing.

As I walked toward the sink, I felt like I was walking up to my own coffin. The other end of the line was dead silent, and I realized both of us were holding our breath.

But I knew.

Somehow I just knew even before I saw the little pink plus that it would be there staring up at me. Mocking me like a cruel joke.

I wanted to faint, and again the world went dizzy, and I sank onto the bathroom floor.

"Piper?" Hailey whispered.

"Millions of women try to get pregnant every day and can't," I said, my voice hollow.

"They do, but that doesn't mean you have to..."

"It might not be millions. Maybe it's only thousands. But still, they all try, and they all want a baby so badly."

"Piper, that doesn't mean—"

"I should be grateful," I said. "I should be happy."

"You're pregnant," Hailey said. It wasn't a question.

Not anymore.

"I don't know how I'm going to tell him."

"Let's worry about him later. For now, I want to think

about you," my sister said. "Are you sure you want this?"

I pressed a hand to my stomach and leaned back against the bathroom wall. This place, this city. It had all been part of my fresh start. In his way, even Jackson had been part of that.

And now all of that was going to change. Again.

But I still knew the answer to her question without thinking. I'd always wanted children. Of course, in my daydreams, I'd been married first.

"Yes," I said. "I want this baby."

"I know this isn't how you wanted it to be, but for what it's worth, I always thought you'd be a great mother," Piper offered softly.

"Thank you." I still felt numb. The cold bathroom floor was all I could feel, aside from my racing heart. My palms were growing sweaty, and before my phone slipped from my hand, I cleared my throat and said, "Look, I think I'm going to lie down for a little while. Could I call you back later?"

"Sure, of course," Hailey said.

"And one other thing," I said.

"What's that?"

"Don't tell Mom about this either. Not yet."

"Of course not," Hailey replied swiftly. "But hey."

"Yeah?"

"I love you. And I meant what I said."

"I love you too." I hung up the phone, crawled toward my bed, and climbed beneath the sheets, hoping they would swallow me whole.

I was going to have a baby. Jackson's baby.

Distantly, I wondered if the baby would have his piercing

eyes or silky dark hair. Whether I was carrying a boy or a girl.

But it was all too soon for that and all too surreal.

I couldn't think about the baby or who I would tell or even when I would go to the doctor.

It was too much. And for now?

I was just going to lie in my bed and cry like my heart was breaking. Because the second I told Jackson about this baby, I was going to lose him.

CHAPTER SEVENTEEN

JACKSON

I blew a sigh out my nose and resisted the urge to pound at the keyboard until all my frustration had finally dissipated. After all my work, all my hours of negotiations, compromises, and number crunching, the investors I'd lined up wanted to back out of the merger.

It didn't make any goddamned sense, and that alone was enough to make me want to rip my hair from my scalp. Worse, I had to deal with every inane, bullet-pointed excuse on my own since Piper had taken the day off for a doctor's visit.

Briefly, I considered calling her and asking her to reschedule her appointment to a more convenient time. Like, say, when the world wasn't coming down around our ears. But I knew that wasn't an option.

I was going to have to ride this wave alone, no matter how choppy—and stupid—the waters.

Slowly, I rolled my tongue over my teeth and opened a new document, typing quickly and carefully, though I was sure to retain a civil and respectful tone.

Maybe Piper could at least look this over before I sent it. Make sure we were heading in the right direction. After all, anyone who'd met me knew I wasn't exactly the kind of guy who knew how to handle people with more delicate sensibilities than my own.

Pulling my phone from my pocket, I shot her a quick text asking if there was any way she might be able to come in just for an hour or two, and in a matter of seconds the phone buzzed in my hand.

Sure. Be there soon.

Good. That was something at least. With Piper by my side, I'd be able to talk the investors into just about anything. And, knowing her, she'd be sure to color-code their responses.

In spite of everything, I smiled to myself, glanced at the board she'd made for me, and then settled back into my work. In such a short span of time, work had become more than just the struggle to maintain my success. Now, every day that I checked a new item off the list or followed her carefully laid plans, I felt like I was doing something to make her proud.

Like we were a team. And the more time went on, the more I felt like I didn't want to do any of this without her. In fact, I was beginning to wonder how anything had ever gotten done before she'd come along.

Twenty minutes into my attempt at drafting the perfect memo, there was a gentle knock at my office door. I blew out a sigh of relief.

"Come in," I called, not bothering to look up from my work. "Piper, come here and read this."

The door clicked closed, and the smell of her lavender perfume along with her soft footfalls made me aware of her approach. I breathed deep, letting her general presence flood me for a moment before pointing at the screen.

"These bastards want to cancel the merger. After everything we've done."

"Oh." Her voice sounded hollow, and I glanced up at her. "That's awful," she added.

I frowned as I took in her appearance. Was she normally so pale, or was it just the soft glow of the computer screen that made her skin look chalkier than I'd ever seen it before?

"What happened at the doctor's?" I asked, my stomach clenching suddenly. What a shit. I hadn't even asked her why she was going or if she was all right. *Jesus, don't let it be something serious.* "Are you feeling all right?"

"I'm feeling fine. Just a checkup," she murmured and then glanced at me, meeting my eyes for only a second before her pupils darted back to my computer screen again.

"There's no way you can send this email," she sighed, a little of the color seeming to return to her cheeks as she focused on the job at hand.

"Why not?" I demanded.

"Because you sound like you're negotiating with a supervillain rather than the people who you are hoping to partner with." Her mouth thinned into a line, and she rolled my chair back, pushing me away so she could get closer to the keyboard. "We just need to soften up some of this language," she added.

"The language is plenty soft," I mumbled, but it was all bluster. I was just glad she was here and that everything was all right. If she needed to fix my email, so be it.

"Maybe for a hostage negotiator," she shot back.

I watched as she studied my words, clicking here and there as she nipped and tucked my sentences. Still, as she went, she didn't seem to have that same laser-focused determination she always had when she set to a task. She hadn't made a single complaint about my grammar or anything.

Weird.

"Piper, there's something wrong," I said.

She glanced in my direction but still didn't quite meet my gaze.

"What's that?" she asked.

"You tell me. Your forehead is wrinkled like you're trying to diffuse a bomb."

She sighed. "I thought you wanted me to fix this for you."

"Was it something at the doctor that you're not telling me?"

"Jackson..." she started, but I couldn't let her go on. I couldn't let her push me away.

"Just answer the question."

"Did it ever occur to you that some things are personal?" she shot back. "Stop pushing me."

"You're the one making me push," I countered. "If there's something wrong..."

"Nobody makes you push. You just...do. And there is nothing wrong, all right? Just a regular female checkup, and sometimes you feel a little off afterward. Jeez." She shook her head and then clicked the mouse button. "Now read the email."

I moved closer to the screen, reading her words with only half my attention. The rest of it was focused solely on

153

the tension that now crackled in the air between us and the way she crossed her arms over her chest and tapped her shoe against the floor as I read.

"This is exactly what I needed. Thanks."

"You're welcome," she said with a forced smile. "Now, if that's all, I'm going to get back to my day off and relax a little."

"No, you're not," I said, laying a hand on her arm as she stood. "Something is different, I can tell. And you're not leaving until we talk about it."

I knew it was unreasonable, but I was past giving a shit. The merger falling apart was bad enough, and now I couldn't help but wonder if the doctor's appointment was just an excuse for her to take the day off because something had changed between us.

Was she over me?

The thought sliced through me like a blade, and when she shook my hand off her, I didn't try to stop her.

"I'm done discussing this," she said. "I've gone through the proper channels to take a day off, and that's what I'm going to do, Jackson."

Without another word, she stalked toward the door and opened it, disappearing behind the frosted glass.

I couldn't seem to shake the strange and awful sense that it might be for the last time, which was ridiculous. I was overtired and stressed with work, that was all. When Piper was ready to tell me what was bothering her, she would. In the meantime, I needed to focus on getting this merger back on track, or we could both be out of a job.

I turned back to my computer, but the dull sense of dread

stayed with me long after that door closed.

CHAPTER EIGHTEEN

PIPER

The whole walk home from the office, I had to remind myself to keep putting one foot in front of the other. I was dizzy and nauseated, and my head was spinning at the speed of sound, but whether it was because of the pregnancy or simply because of Jackson, I didn't know.

Pregnant.

Dear God, what was I going to do?

My paranoia—my absolute certainty that he had read the truth in my face—was too much for me to bear, and I found myself searching for a bench and sucking down desperate gulps of air that were quickly becoming hard to come by.

When I reached a bus stop, I huddled into the little glass enclosure and sat down, grateful for the lack of company as I drew a deep breath.

There was no denying it now. No running from the truth. The doctor had taken the tests and shown me the pictures, and the truth was right there on the screen. There was a little pea-sized person inside me.

A person depending on me to make the right choices for the rest of their future.

And the fact of the matter was, the best decision I could make was to ensure this baby would be cared for by people who loved him or her unconditionally.

It was true I hadn't planned on being a mother, but when I'd stared at that image, I'd known the truth. There were no options for me, no other choices to be made. From the second I knew I was pregnant, this baby was completely and irrevocably mine.

I wouldn't give this baby up for all the world. And I wouldn't make him or her live with a father who didn't feel the same way—nor would I force Jackson into a life of caring for a child he'd been so open and certain about not wanting.

So today had been the day where I had to make my choice once and for all.

I thought once I saw him I would know. That the answer would be so clear to me that all my doubts and restless thoughts about what to tell him would be laid to rest.

But no. Just like everything else in this relationship, it hadn't been so easy.

I looked into his eyes, if only for an instant, and saw that cold, calculating look of his. That desperation for his business to succeed. That was what drove him, what got him up in the morning. A child would only derail that, and I couldn't bear it for him to resent the baby or me. But, shit, it would hurt to walk away.

A few times, I'd thought of turning on my heel and telling him everything, pouring out my heart and soul—my terror, my joy, my utter shock—but every time I came close, he would bark something else at me. Another demand. Another question I wasn't ready to answer.

Because with him, everything was on his terms.

Always.

And then, when he'd tried to press me one last time? Well, that was as close to an answer as I could have gotten. He was uncompromising, stubborn, and used to being in control. A baby would require changes on all fronts. Living life on his terms twenty-four-seven would be over.

So my choice was made. I couldn't tell him about the baby. Which meant from now on, absolutely everything had to change.

I had to leave this city and my fresh start behind me for an even newer, fresher start. I had to go home to be with my parents. They wouldn't understand—hell, they probably wouldn't support me, either—but they'd raised two kids, which made them perfect candidates for helping me with this new chapter of my life.

I would feel like a loser, coming back home unmarried, jobless, and pregnant, but my baby would have a soft place to fall.

And right now? That was all that mattered.

With another rush of nausea, I crumpled on the cold bus stop seat and waved off the driver of the bus that was pulling to a stop in front of me.

I still needed this. Some time alone without the reality of my apartment or my job or my future. There was so much to do, so much to plan, and I wasn't so sure all my organizational systems would come to the rescue this time.

After all, no matter how regimented my planning was, I

couldn't magically come up with money for a crib and diapers and baby toys. And before that, maternity clothes and doctor's visits and a million other things I probably didn't know about yet.

Closing my eyes, I forced myself to breathe deep in through my nose and out through my mouth until my heartbeat steadied again.

I just had to look at today as the start of a new chapter. A new book, even.

Jackson would close out the end of my old life. When my baby asked about his father... Well, that was another chapter's problem.

For today, I'd have to think of what I needed to do.

With a shaking hand, I grasped my phone and dialed the number I'd been dreading almost as much as Jackson's.

The phone rang once, twice, and then the clipped, cool tones I knew so well greeted me.

"Piper," my mother said.

"Mom." My voice shook. I couldn't help it.

"What's wrong?"

My heart is breaking.

My life is over.

I'm totally overwhelmed.

The answers spun through my mind, and finally I landed on my truth.

"Everything." I choked out the word as a sob rose up my throat. "Everything is wrong. I need to come home."

CHAPTER NINETEEN

JACKSON

The next morning, as soon as I got in to work, I stared at my door, waiting for Piper to finally arrive. She may have gotten away from me yesterday, but today I was going to have the answers I'd been looking for that had kept me up half the fucking night.

I'd messaged her. I'd called her. And nothing. Which left me sitting at home remembering the worn, weary look in her eyes as she'd surveyed my email. Her guarded, tense tone.

Something must have happened that she wasn't telling me about, and I was going to find out what.

So, when the clock struck nine and the elevator doors opened with their soft, metallic ping, I was already waiting with my hands folded on my desk for Piper to enter and pour me my morning cup of coffee.

But she didn't.

Instead, another fifteen minutes went by. Then another. And then it was nine thirty and I had no coffee, no assistant, and no clue.

Snatching my phone from the surface of my desk, I checked for some sort of notice that Piper might be in late today, but no messages awaited.

Frowning, I opened a new conversation window and started typing, but just before I hit Send, I heard the click of my door as it opened. I looked up to find an ashen-faced Piper staring at me, her knuckles white as she clutched the doorknob.

"You're late," I said.

She nodded. "Yes. And I'm sorry about that. Do you have time to talk?"

I glanced at my calendar, pretending I hadn't already cleared my morning to speak with her, because I was in a foul mood and was an asshole like that.

"I can find some time," I said. "Sit down."

"That won't be necessary. I won't be long."

I raised my eyebrows, and then my gaze fell to her clothes. Unlike her usual business attire, she was wearing jeans and a button-down blouse. Her purse was still slung over one shoulder, and she hitched it higher as she finally released the door and closed it behind her.

"I'm hoping you came in here with some answers," I said.

She frowned. "Look, Jackson, I don't know what—"

"You came in here yesterday looking like you'd seen a ghost, and then you left without explanation. You didn't answer my messages," I said, my concern and fear bubbling up into anger on a dime again.

"I was busy." She wrung her hands in front of her before crossing her arms protectively over her chest.

"Doing what?" I demanded.

"Look, that's not what I want to talk about," she said.

"If only you were in a situation where you were the boss.

Since you're not—"

"I quit," she cut in, her words clipped and to the point.

Her words hung in the air between us, and I could barely get my head around them. She didn't sound angry. If anything, I might have thought she was on the verge of tears, but she took a steadying breath and clasped her hands in front of her again.

"I'm sorry it has to be so sudden, but I have to quit."

"Did you find a better job? I don't understand," I said, my mind reeling.

How could she go from redesigning an entire department, taking on more responsibility, and revolutionizing a company to leaving it in one fell swoop? I started again, trying to make heads or tails of what she'd said. "You know I value your input here. If I asked too much of you during the merger..."

She shook her head. "It has nothing to do with you or the merger, I promise."

I raised my eyebrows, thinking through my options as the thought of her leaving hit me like a two-by-four to the skull. "Well then if it has nothing to do with me, the rest of our arrangement—"

"Will also have to end," she finished, her tone choked now. "I'm leaving the city."

It was like a sucker punch to the solar plexus, and I sucked in a breath. "Piper, I don't understand. If you got a new job, you know I would pay you more. What is it you need? Name your price."

She shook her head, her bottom lip quivering now. "This isn't about a price. And it's not you either, I swear. I just need to be with my family for a while. I'm homesick."

"Then I'll fly you to see them. Don't be so drastic. This can still work."

She took a shaky breath. "It's not something a quick visit can fix."

"And how can you be so sure?"

"Because..." She swallowed hard. "Because there's an emergency. With my sister. I have to be with her, and I have to focus on doing what's right for my family right now."

I blinked. "Is there something I can do to help? Does she need a specialist? Is this why you had to go to the doctor? Does she have some genetic disease you needed to be tested for?"

"Jackson, I can't talk about it. Please, for once, don't try to micromanage the situation, okay? I need to leave, and you need to let me. End of story."

This was nonsense. No matter where she was, I could find a way to be with her. If only she'd just let me in and tell me what was going on.

She blew out a trembling sigh, and for a second, the Piper I knew reared her head. I could see the affection in her eyes and the sadness too. "We both know you're not the long-distance type. We had fun together. Why can't you just let that be enough?"

"Because it's not," I argued. "It's not enough for me. I'm not willing to let you just walk away with barely an explanation about what I can do or how I can help."

"That's because there is nothing you can do. The best thing you can do for me is let me start my life over somewhere new. To let me leave you here, where you belong." She sniffled and then swiped a hand over her face. "And to promise me you won't come looking for me."

"No," I said solemnly. "I deserve more than just this pathetic explanation, Piper."

"And I'm not willing to give that to you," she said, her voice cold and stony for the first time since she'd begun to speak. "Goodbye, Jackson."

She strode toward the door for the second time in as many days, leaving me broken in her wake.

CHAPTER TWENTY

JACKSON

No.

This wasn't happening.

I wasn't going to *allow* it to happen.

I gripped the edge of my desk and propelled myself from my chair and crossed the room in three easy strides before flinging my door open again. The people in the cubicles nearest my office all turned to look, but I ignored them, scanning the aisles instead for the pretty dark-red wave of hair I knew so well.

When I found her, though, she was turning, facing the metal doors of the elevator as they slid closed in front of her.

"Damn it," I muttered, closing my hands into fists as I stalked toward the stairwell, but even I knew better than to race the elevator.

I could go to her apartment and head her off, but that still didn't guarantee me the answers I was looking for. She clearly wasn't going to give me what I needed. She wasn't ready to talk.

Which left me with no other choice.

Tightening my jaw, I made my way to Human Resources and stopped short in front of Clara's desk.

She looked up at me, her gray eyebrows tilting in curiosity.

"I need the keys to the file room," I said.

"Right away," she croaked. She opened a metal drawer beside her and grabbed a little ring of keys.

"Which ones go to the personnel files?"

"The personnel files?" she parroted back to me.

"Yes," I snapped. I didn't have time for this. I needed answers, and I needed them now. There was only the slightest chance my plan would work, and I had to get it in motion as quickly as I could muster.

"The blue one," Clara said. "It'll be the stack closest to the door."

"Thank you," I murmured and then paced the length of the floor until I got to the file room, all too aware of the way each of my employee's eyes followed me as I went. I wanted to snap at them to get back to their business, but I couldn't bring myself to slow down enough to bother—not when I had something more important on the line.

I shut the door behind me, pulled the ancient rope that turned on the file room's dim light, and stuck the blue key into the nearest filing cabinet.

Quickly, I riffled through the alphabetical lettering until I reached the name I needed and snatched up Piper's file, my heart pounding in my chest.

This was it. The moment of truth.

I flipped open the file and thumbed past the insurance and social security information until I found her emergency contact form. The first person listed was her mother. The second?

Her sister, Hailey.

Boom.

My heart leapt into my throat, and I pulled my phone from my pocket, quickly dialing her number with shaking, anxious fingers. The phone rang once, twice, and then a dial tone sounded.

The number I reached had been disconnected.

"Damn it," I swore again. She must have gotten a new phone. But how likely was it that she had gotten a new address?

I glanced at the information, weighing the options again in my mind.

Piper had walked away and asked me to stay out of it, but I knew for a fact that her family couldn't possibly have the resources I had available to me. If something was wrong with Hailey—and if that something was bothering Piper—who better than I to fix it? I had to help.

By rights, Piper didn't even need to know it was me behind it. I could just go talk to Hailey in person, find out what was wrong, and fix everything, with Piper being none the wiser.

Nodding to myself, I copied Hailey's address onto the notepad on my phone and then strode back to my office and booked a flight. In the morning I would have my answers. And just maybe I could find a way to win Piper back too.

♦ ♦ ♦ ♦

When my plane landed in Chicago two days later, I made quick work of grabbing my luggage and renting a car. I hadn't bothered to book a hotel room—I couldn't imagine I would be in town long enough for that, but as I drove into the township where Piper had grown up, I couldn't help but envy her a little.

Sprawling trees lined the suburban streets, and the playground of the elementary school was packed with laughing, screaming children. It seemed like the kind of place where kids could wander off and have adventures. The kind of place to have a happy, safe childhood.

I could picture her here, growing up and becoming the person I had come to care for. The woman I now realized I'd fallen for.

Swallowing that thought, I turned on a few streets until I reached a little development of cottages and slowed, trying to find the number I'd memorized on the plane ride.

But I didn't need to bother.

I knew the house instantly.

Not from the number or the woman who looked just like Piper but from the car parked in the driveway.

Piper's car.

My heart plummeted into my stomach, and I considered driving away and coming back when I could have Hailey's attention to myself. Piper, whether I liked it or not, didn't want to see me, and I knew forcing this issue was wrong. Still, once I knew she was there, I couldn't seem to stop myself. It was like my brain went offline and my heart was working on autopilot. It was a feeling that was entirely fucking new to me.

I parked behind Piper's car, walking carefully up the long drive while the early afternoon sun warmed my skin.

Distantly, I could hear voices from the open window.

"You really didn't need to do this. It's too much," Piper was saying softly.

A second, higher-pitched voice responded. "Oh, it was the least I could do. I figured you have enough to worry about right now. One less expense is always a good thing."

"Not just that, sis," Piper said. "All of this." There was a long pause, and I slowed, my stomach dropping into my feet as her voice sounded tear-filled. "Taking me, *us*, in. It's more than I could have ever expected."

I frowned, the words not computing. But then, as I rounded the shrubs, I understood her meaning, and it rocked me to my core.

Through the wide bay window, I could see the mostly assembled crib in the center of the room. Piper was standing beside it, one hand on the railing as she glanced at the mobile, the other resting low on her flat belly.

One less expense...

Taking us *in...*

Cold realization sank deep in my chest, freezing my heart and pausing its beat.

Piper was pregnant. With my baby.

I was frozen to the spot, staring at her through the glass as her gaze slowly centered on mine.

CHAPTER TWENTY-ONE

PIPER

The moment I saw him, the world whooshed around me in a blur of color and light and sound. Distantly, I heard my sister asking me what was wrong, but then she followed my gaze out the wide bay window to spy the tall, handsome man standing on her garden path.

"Is that...?" she asked, but I was too busy gulping down my next breath to answer her. The air was thinner than I remembered and harder to come by.

And then, all at once, my panic was gone. Replaced instead with white-hot boiling anger.

Why was he here?

My stomach twisted, and I clenched my teeth, balling my hands at my sides as it sank in why he was here—what he must have done. I'd told him specifically to stay out of it, that we were finished, and he'd ignored me because that's what he did. He barreled over people's wants and needs. I relished the anger that overshadowed the pain of heartbreak and held it close and tight.

Stepping away from the crib, I crossed the room and swung open the front door, marching down the front path until

I was only a few feet from him.

"What are you doing here?" I demanded.

For a moment he said nothing, and a new, strange expression crossed his face. It wasn't his usual stern, business demeanor or his angry, tough-guy act. It was almost something like...hurt.

His voice was tight when he finally answered, "I could ask you the same thing."

"What do you mean? This is my sister's house. I don't owe you any explanations."

"Don't you?" His voice was cold now, and his gaze flicked to the window behind me, where the crib and mobile still sat, a massive admission of my guilt.

"That's Hailey's," I lied a little too quickly.

"I heard you," he said simply and then waited as I let the truth wash over me.

He knew. I'd been caught red-handed. My heart sank into my stomach, and I clutched the space there, certain the baby could feel my rioting emotions.

"You have no right to be here," I tried again. "I told you to stay away."

"And what right did you have to do that?" he demanded, his voice rising slightly now. "What right did you have to keep me from my child? To not tell me?"

"We both know I was making the right decision," I shot back.

"For who? For you? You wanted to raise a child who would never know his father?" He speared a hand through his hair and blew out a long breath. "You're unbelievable. All the lies... You had me thinking your sister was sick. I came all this way to help her. To help you."

"Nobody asked you to do that," I said. "In fact, I recall pleading with you to do just the opposite."

"Maybe you didn't ask, but that's what good people do. They help the people they love. They don't lie to them over and over and fucking over again, Piper." He was yelling now, but I was too distracted by his words to say anything.

The word "love" had shot through me like an arrow, piercing the empty space where my heart used to be.

"Say something. Defend yourself at least," he demanded.

"Y-You love me?" I whispered.

"I thought I did." His gaze was like a glacier. "But now I realize I don't even fucking know you. How could I love the woman who tried to keep my child from me and then stands by her choice when she gets caught?"

I swallowed hard. "Jackson—"

"No, save it, Piper. There's nothing you can say or do that will make this okay."

"I thought about telling you," I tried. "But I know how you feel about children, and I thought you would be better off..."

"How nice of you to make the choice for me," he spat. "You know what? You'll be hearing from my lawyer, and I only want to hear from yours. I can't even stand to look at you right now."

He glowered at me with full, unadulterated fury, and I stared back, my lips pursed as I crossed my arms over my chest. There was nothing I could say or do to fix this. No way I could make what I'd done make sense. Not to him. Not when he was like this. Hell, maybe never.

So instead, I stood there, heartsick, watching as he marched back to his car. Before he got inside, though, he stared back at me, his eyes icy.

"I have a right to be in my child's life, and I will. Whatever it takes, Piper. So don't think this is the last of this."

With that, he climbed into the car and reversed onto the street, speeding off in a plume of exhaust and hatred.

All the while, I stood stock still, watching him go and dealing with my own tangled mess of feelings. My hurt at the way he'd looked at me, the anger that he'd meddled, my frustration that he would never understand.

But most of all, my heartbreak. He'd loved me... Loved me enough to want to fix my problems even after I'd cast him aside. And I...

I thought of that night on the rooftop garden. Our trip to the museum, all those lunches and dinners shared in his office. The few rare times I'd gotten to really see him for who he was.

Those moments when my heart shone like a thousand bits of light.

I loved him too. And now he would never know it. Our child might never know it, but I did. I loved him with all my heart.

Which was why I'd tried to spare him all of this.

But now, after everything, I was the one standing here, my head in my hands, having lost every last piece of my life.

I heard the door open again behind me, and I knew my sister was watching me from the porch.

"You heard?" I asked lifelessly.

"Yeah. I'm so very sorry, sis."

"Me too," I replied, a wedge of emotion clogging my throat. "Me too."

CHAPTER TWENTY–TWO

PIPER

For a long while, we were silent. Hailey stood over the tea kettle, watching as the water began to steam, and I sat at her little round kitchen table, my hands folded in front of me.

I studied every detail of them, every line along my knuckles, every vein beneath the skin. Anything to keep my mind from Jackson and the way he'd looked at me when he'd sped away.

Anything to keep me from what felt like a never-ending rush of humiliation and shame.

The high-pitched scream of the kettle sounded, and I closed my eyes, listening to the burble of water as Hailey poured water into mugs.

"Green or Earl Grey?" she asked in a muted tone.

"You have decaf? The caffeine isn't good for the baby."

"Oh, right. Still getting used to...well, yeah. Give me a second." She rummaged in her drawers and then snapped one shut before I heard the soft thud of her feet on the linoleum floor and then the gentle scrape of the wooden chair as it slid backward.

"Open your eyes. Nothing to hide from here," Hailey said,

and I looked up to find her placing a mug in front of me.

Turning, she grabbed some sugar and milk from the island in the middle of her dated, cherry kitchen and thunked them onto the middle of the matching table.

"Okay," she sighed. "Now, let's have some tea and talk about what might make you feel better. Maybe we could talk baby names? I like Tallulah, personally."

I shook my head, wrapping my chilled hands around the scalding cup in front of me.

"I'm not sure anything is going to make me feel better. I mean, how could he just *leave* like that?" Gripping the string of my tea bag, I plunked it up and down and then stared down into the darkening water.

"Like, he wants to prove that he's going to be here for this baby, but the second he finds out I'm pregnant, he's back on the road again?" I let out a humorless laugh. "Frankly, it's exactly what I expected from him. I shouldn't be surprised."

Silence reigned between us, broken only by the soft clatter of Hailey's spoon as she stirred her tea.

I counted the seconds. One, two, three, and then I glanced at her, determined to make her meet my gaze. When she didn't, I spoke again.

"Well?" I prompted.

"Well." She sighed. "Look, I don't want to upset you any more. We can talk about this when you've had a little time."

"I don't need time. I want to know what you think," I said.

Hailey frowned and then sipped her drink. With another sigh, she started again. "Well, I can kind of see where he's coming from, honestly. I mean, what was he supposed to do?

Throw his arms open and ask your due date? The guy got blindsided."

"That's no excuse," I said.

"I think it might be." She chewed on her bottom lip. "You've had a couple of days to deal with this news and process how it's going to affect your life. Jackson didn't have that. He just found out that not only were you pregnant, but you lied to him about it repeatedly to keep him from finding out."

"Because he doesn't want children!" I argued. "I did this *for* him. If you could've heard how he spoke about having a baby..."

"That was ancient history, Piper. His opinion could have changed in the last decade. And besides, would that be your assumption if you were in his shoes right now?" Hailey asked patiently. "Or would you think the person didn't tell you because you were lacking somehow? Because, for whatever reason, they didn't think you'd be a good influence in their child's life?"

I frowned, that noxious sickly feeling returning to my stomach. "I hadn't thought about it that way. If he'd just asked, or let me speak, I would have explained why I didn't tell him."

"He was in shock, I imagine. He didn't know this was the kind of conversation he'd be having today, I guarantee that," Hailey said. Then she reached toward me, took my hand, and stroked the back of my fingers.

"Look, Piper, you made a choice. You thought it was the right thing to do, but the thing is, you made that choice without his consent or knowledge. Like it or not, that's going to be a tough thing for a guy like Jackson to swallow."

I gripped my sister's hand and squeezed. "Did you hear the part...the part where he said he loved me?" I choked out the words.

She nodded. "I did."

"I love him too, you know. I wouldn't have worried about ruining his life if I didn't love him. I wouldn't have..." Hot tears scratched at the back of my throat, and I swallowed hard.

"I know," Hailey said. "I know."

"So what do I do now? I can't get him back. I can't force him to stay with me because I'm having this baby. Not after everything I've done."

Hailey frowned. "No, but you can give him what he thinks he wants right now."

"Which is?" I prompted.

Hailey took another sip of her tea, her brow furrowing as she thought. "Well, what do you think you would want if you were in his shoes?"

"I guess...reassurance more than anything. But it's not like I can call him and leave a message or something."

"Then don't. Go back to the city and do something about this."

My mind whirled. "He won't want to see me."

"Then don't let him. Leave him a letter or something. Just, you know, let him know that what happened doesn't have anything to do with him. Not really."

I nodded. "I can do that."

"I know you can."

"And what if he still hates me when he's done reading it?"

"Then the two of you will work it out. Because right now?

This isn't about either of you. This is about little Tallulah."

"I hate that name." I grinned.

"I knew you would." Hailey patted my hand. "Now go get to work, tiger."

CHAPTER TWENTY-THREE

JACKSON

Twice in my life I'd thought I was going to be a father.

The first time, I was sure my life would fall apart. I had barely started a company and was with a girl I barely knew and certainly didn't love. The prospect of spending the rest of time with her crushed me. The idea of being a father was hardly ever on my mind, to be honest.

In truth, I spent my time thinking about what my days with her would be like. The sort of mindless rhythm we'd fall into as two people bound together not by love but by our responsibility to the life that depended on us.

It was true that when the miscarriage had happened, I'd been relieved. But now, as I thought again about being a father, of having that new precious life in my care, I wondered if my reality had changed in the years that had passed since then.

Because now, when I thought of this child, I didn't think about the responsibility like a sort of crushing weight on my freedom. Instead, I looked around my cold, unfeeling apartment and realized the warmth of a child—of a family— was exactly what I needed.

Barely twenty-four hours had passed, and already I was

imagining where to put the cradle, what I needed to get rid of, what sorts of things I'd need to read up on. I wasn't scared. I wasn't anxious. In spite of being angry and devastated by the loss of Piper and her lies...

I was excited.

Truly, deeply excited at the idea of taking my child to Central Park to play chess or catch. To help him with his homework and put him to bed at night.

Before, I had been broken. The kind of person who wouldn't make a child's life any better, no matter how hard I tried.

But now? I was someone new. Someone different.

And that was because of Piper.

I sat back on my sofa and took a deep breath. Naturally, I couldn't think about the baby without thinking of her. Would he have her same dark-red locks and heart-shaped face? Would he laugh like her or have her keen sense of organization?

I also couldn't help but think of Piper. Was she taking care of herself? Eating well? Sleeping enough?

I couldn't bring myself to ask her, nor could I think of her without my chest tightening and my hands balling into fists.

I couldn't understand it. Or worse, maybe I could.

Maybe she'd seen me for the broken, heartless corporate man I was and had deemed me unable to care for a child. Whatever had gone through her head, it must have been bad enough to not only leave me but to take my child away without me ever knowing about them.

And then, when I thought of her face... The way she'd paled when she'd finally been caught out.

Like a victim facing their abuser.

I pinched my nose between thumb and forefinger and took another deep breath as guilt hammered at my chest.

I couldn't think about that now. Soon I would have to get my lawyer involved and see what sort of custody arrangement we could work out.

No matter what, I was going to have to see her again. To bring her back to the city for her doctor's appointments and to speak with her about the kind of life we would develop together for our child.

Rather than feeling trapped by the idea of her, though, I felt like I was missing a limb. Like seeing her again would make me feel all the love, all the need, all the completeness I was desperate to shove back down. I couldn't forgive her, not after everything she'd done. But if I saw her again...

Well, how could I turn her away?

I couldn't. Because the fact of the matter was that I still loved her. Heart, body, mind, and soul, I still loved her, and there was nothing even my most determined thoughts could do to change that.

Flexing my fingers, I pushed myself off the sofa just in time to hear the gentle *whoosh* of something as it slid across my floor.

I frowned, following the sound until I found a white envelope with my name scrawled on it in perfectly neat, very familiar handwriting. There was no address. Even if there were, I knew the mail carrier would never deliver a letter like that.

I picked it up, strode to the door, and swung it open just as

Piper was pressing the elevator button in the hall.

"Stop," I called out, my pulse hammering.

She spun around, her cheeks a full flush of color and her ponytail nearly hitting her in the face.

"Everything is in the letter," she murmured, her eyes glassy with tears. "You said you didn't want to see me, and... well, I want to respect your wishes."

The way I hadn't respected hers, my conscience repeated.

The elevator dinged open behind her, but I held up a hand.

"Save me the suspense since you're here. What's it say?" I asked, holding the envelope up.

"I..." She twisted her fingers in front of her. "I had sort of planned on you reading it. But, you know, it's just...it's a custody agreement I drew up. I wanted you to know that no matter what happens between us, you'll never have to fight to see your child. What happened, what I did—that wasn't because of you. When I found out I was pregnant, I couldn't stop thinking of that day at the museum when you told me you never wanted to have children and how stuck you felt and..."

She shook her head. "It's put much more eloquently in the letter. The fact is, I didn't want to force you into something you didn't want just because I was pregnant, but I know now that it should have been your choice. I'm sorry. But really, I want to respect what you want and I'm going to go. I promise."

"Don't you dare." I took a few more steps into the hall and then showed her the envelope before I tore it in two.

"Jackson—" she gasped.

"I don't want any custody agreement," I said. "I want to have a family, and I want that with you. It was selfless, what you did. You were ready to raise this baby alone to protect me, and I..."

I shook my head, struggling to find the words. "That's why I love you so much. You're so brave. But you know what? You and this baby are mine, and you're not going anywhere. Never again, you understand?"

She nodded, tears welling in the corner of her eyes. "I love you, you know," she said.

"I do know. And you should know that this is my choice. Not because you're having my baby, but because this is what I want. A life with you and with little whoever he or she is."

She nodded. "Then you can have it. Forever."

"Forever," I murmured. "I like the sound of that."

EPILOGUE

PIPER

"Would you hand me that stack of folders?" I asked my sweet husband.

We now shared the corner office that had once been the location of so many illicit encounters. I'd been promoted to junior executive—and not because I was fucking the boss. I'd refused for nearly two years until I was certain I'd earned the job title. But thank goodness it had been mostly a non-affair with our staff. Anyone with a set of working eyeballs could tell how perfect we were together. I was praised often and thoroughly for how well I had *tamed the dragon*. And not to mention, the merger we'd worked so hard on together went through without a hitch.

"Of course." Jackson rose to his feet and set the stack of folders on the desk in front of me. But as soon as he sat back down, his eyes darted to his computer screen again.

"What are you doing?" He seemed so distracted this morning.

A glance over at Jackson's work station revealed what I suspected all along. He was watching our daughter again.

While I was away on maternity leave, Jackson had

surprised me by remodeling the office building to add a brand-new daycare facility for the office staff. Now all three of us came to work together, occasionally had lunch together, and the built-in security cameras played almost nonstop on Jackson's computer screen. And if Mommy or Daddy had to work late, we'd bring Mae up to our office, where we'd order in dinner and let her play on the rug with the basket of toys we kept in the filing cabinet. It was a pretty sweet setup.

"She's just waking up from a nap." He smiled that smile of pure joy I'd come to love—the one he seemed to save just for Mae and me. I didn't think I'd ever tire of it.

It was sweet how passionate Jackson was about keeping us all close. And for a man I was convinced didn't want a child—well, let's just say he's already trying to knock me up again. It'd taken some work on his part, but he'd eventually won over my parents and Hailey. They'd accepted and welcomed him like the family he'd never had. My exacting alpha-male CEO of a husband turned into one big softie, and my misadventures with the boss ended up leading me to a lifetime of happiness.

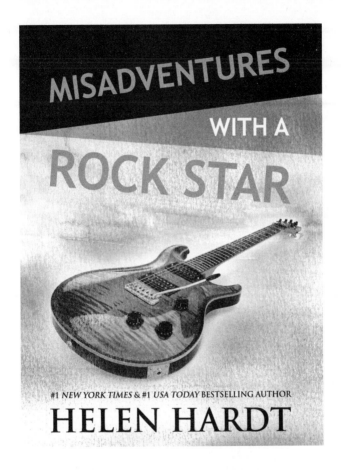

CHAPTER ONE

JETT

Janet and Lindy tongued each other in a sloppy, openmouthed kiss. Lindy, platinum-blond with fair skin, smoothed her hand over the strap of ebony-haired Janet's soft-pink camisole before pulling it down and freeing one of her plump, dark tits. Her nipple was a deep violet, and Lindy skimmed her fingers over its tip before giving it a pinch.

Janet let out a low moan, sucked Lindy's bottom lip into her mouth, and released her creamy tits from the scant blue tube top she wore. They kissed each other more frantically, groaning, pinching and twisting each other's nipples.

"That's hot, man," Zane said, stroking the bulge under his jeans.

Zane Michaels was the keyboardist for our band, Emerald Phoenix. I loved him like a brother, but he hadn't matured past his teen years. I couldn't deny the ladies looked great, but this wasn't anything I hadn't witnessed many times before.

Lindy was now nestled between Janet's firm thighs, her pink tongue sliding between the folds of Janet's purple pussy. Zane looked about to explode.

And I couldn't have cared less.

Oh, Janet and Lindy were hot as hell. I'd had them separately and together, and they both gave killer blowjobs and let me fuck not only their pussies but their tight asses as well. Janet loved to be handcuffed to the bed, and Lindy let me spank her as hard as I liked.

Tonight, though? I wasn't interested.

Same old, same old.

I still had my post-performance high, but I wasn't looking for the usual orgy, despite Janet and Lindy's show and the rest of the scantily clad groupies milling around looking for attention. A redhead was perched on the lap of Bernie Zopes, our drummer, and the backup guitarist, Tony Walker, was getting a BJ from two women who looked like they might be twins.

Nah, couldn't be.

I'd already pushed a few hotties away after one shoved her tongue into my mouth and grabbed my crotch.

"What's with you, man?" Zane had asked.

I hadn't given him a response.

Truthfully, I didn't have one. I just wasn't in the mood. Not for this, anyway.

Zane passed me the joint he was smoking, but I waved it away. I no longer smoked. Bad for my voice. I'd already turned down his flask as well as the many drinks and drugs offered by the chicks in attendance. No booze. Not tonight. And I didn't do anything harder than that.

Not in the fucking mood.

One more concert, and one more drug- and booze- and groupie-filled after-party.

If anyone had told me five years ago I'd be tired of this scene, I would have laughed in his face.

Now?

Janet and Lindy finished their show and stood. Janet strode to Zane and unbuckled his belt, while Lindy walked toward me.

"Hey, Jett. You have way too many clothes on." She cupped my crotch, my lack of erection apparent. "Not happy to see me tonight?"

"Nothing personal, sweetheart. Just not in the mood."

"I always did love a challenge." She nipped at my neck.

"This isn't a challenge."

She pulled back and glared at me with her dark-blue eyes. "*Everything's* a challenge. I want you tonight, and I'm going to have you." She snaked her tongue over my bottom lip.

Well, what the hell? Fucking Lindy was no hardship, and I didn't have anything else pressing to do. My groin began to tighten.

But was it because of the blonde grinding on me? Or the auburn-haired, brown-eyed goddess I caught a glimpse of across the room?

CHAPTER TWO

HEATHER

Several hours earlier...

"I know you love this band," Susie said. "Come on. Please?"

Susie was my roommate and a good friend, but she was a notorious rock and roll groupie. The woman had a pube collection, for God's sake. She'd sworn me to secrecy on that one. She hadn't needed to bother. Who the heck would I tell? Pubic hair didn't regularly come up in conversation. Also, keeping locks of rock stars' gorilla salad in zippered bags made me kind of sick. I'd turned her down when she offered to show it to me.

"Sorry, Suze. Just not up for it tonight."

"I'm so sorry Rod Hanson turned down your rewrite. But sitting around wallowing in self-pity on a Friday night won't make it any better."

"And going to a concert will?"

"A concert *and* an after-party. And watching Jett Draconis and Zane Michaels on stage is an experience every woman should have at least once."

I did love Emerald Phoenix's music, and yes, Jett

Draconis and Zane Michaels were as gorgeous as Greek gods. But...

"Not tonight."

She pulled me off the couch. "Not taking no for an answer. You're going."

◆ ◆ ◆ ◆

Why was I here again?

I stifled a yawn. Watching a couple of women do each other while others undressed, clamoring for a minute of the band's attention, wasn't my idea of a good time. The two women were gorgeous, of course, with tight bodies and big boobs. The contrasts in their skin and hair color made their show even more exotic. They were interesting to watch, but they didn't do much for me sexually. Maybe if I weren't so exhausted. I'd pulled the morning and noon shifts, and my legs were aching.

Even so, I was glad Susie had dragged me to the concert, if only to see and hear Jett Draconis live. His deep bass-baritone was rich enough to fill an opera house but had just enough of a rasp to make him the ultimate rock vocalist. And when he slid into falsetto and then back down to bass notes? Panty-melting. No other words could describe the effect. Watching him had mesmerized me. He lived his music as he sang and played, not as if it were coming from his mouth but emanating from his entire body and soul. The man had been born to perform.

A true artist.

Which only made me feel like more of a loser.

Jett Draconis was my age, had hit the LA scene around the same time I had, and he'd made it big in no time. Me? I was still a struggling screenwriter working a dead-end job waiting tables at a local diner where B-list actors and directors hung out. Not only was I not an A-lister, I wasn't even serving them. When I couldn't sell a movie to second-rate producer Rod Hanson? I hadn't yet said the words out loud, but the time had come to give up.

"What are you doing hanging out here all by yourself?"

Susie's words knocked me out of my barrage of self-pity. For a minute anyway.

"Just bored. Can we leave soon?"

"Are you kidding me? The party's just getting started." She pointed to the two women on the floor. "That's Janet and Lindy. Works every time. They always go home with someone in the band."

"Only proves that men are pigs."

Susie didn't appear to be listening. Her gaze was glued on Zane, the keyboardist, whose gaze was in turn glued on the two women cavorting in the middle of the floor. She turned to me. "Let's make out."

I squinted at her, as if that might help my ears struggling in the loud din. I couldn't possibly have heard her correctly. "What?"

"You and me. Kiss me." She planted a peck right on my mouth.

I stepped away from her. "Are you kidding me?"

"It works. Look around. All the girls do it."

"I'm not a girl. I'm a thirty-year-old woman."

"Don't you think I'm hot?" she asked.

"Seriously? Of course you are." Indeed, Susie looked great with her dark hair flowing down to her ass and her form-fitting leopard-print tank and leggings. "So is Angelina Jolie, but I sure as heck don't want to make out with her. I don't swing that way." Well, for Angelina Jolie I might. Or Lupita Nyong'o. But that was it.

"Neither do I—at least not long-term. But it'll get us closer to the band."

"Is this what you do at all the after-parties you go to?"

She giggled. "Sometimes. But only if there's someone as hot as you to make out with. I have my standards."

Maybe I should have been flattered. But no way was I swapping spit with my friend to get some guy's attention. They were still just men, after all. Even the gorgeous and velvet-voiced Jett Draconis, who seemed to be watching the floor show.

Susie inched toward me again. I turned my head just in time so her lips and tongue swept across my cheek.

"Sorry, girl. If you want to make out, I'm sure there's someone here who will take you up on your offer. Not me, though. It would be too...weird."

She nodded. "Yeah, it would be a little odd. I mean, we live together and all. But I hate that you're just standing here against the wall not having any fun. And I'm not ready to go home yet."

I sighed. This was Susie's scene, and she enjoyed it. She had come to LA for the rockers and was happy to work as a receptionist at a talent agency as long as she made enough money to keep her wardrobe in shape and made enough contacts to get into all the after-parties she wanted. That was the extent of her aspirations. She was living her dream, and she'd no doubt continue to live it until her looks gave out...which wouldn't happen for a while with all the Botox and plastic surgery available in LA. She was a good soul, but right now her ambition was lacking.

"Tell you what," I said. "Have fun. Do your thing. I'll catch an Uber home."

She frowned. "I wanted to show you a good time. I'm sorry I suggested making out. I get a little crazy at these things."

I chuckled. "It's okay. Don't worry about it."

"Please stay. I'll introduce you to some people."

"Any producers or directors here?" I asked.

"I don't know. Mostly the band and their agents, and of course the sound and tech guys who like to try to get it on with the groupies. I doubt any film people are here."

"Then there isn't anyone I need to meet, but thanks for offering." I pulled my phone out of my clutch to check the time. It was nearing midnight, and this party was only getting started.

"Sure I can't convince you to stay?" Susie asked.

"Afraid not." I pulled up the Uber app and ordered a ride. "But have a great time, okay? And stay safe, please."

"I always do." She gave me a quick hug and then lunged toward a group of girls, most of them still dressed, thank God.

I scanned the large room. Susie and her new gaggle of

friends were laughing and drinking cocktails. A couple girls were slobbering over the drummer's dick. The two beautiful women putting on the sex show had abandoned the floor, and the one with dark skin was draped between the legs of Zane Michaels, who was, believe it or not, even prettier than she was. The other sat on Jett Draconis's lap.

Zane Michaels was gorgeous, but Jett Draconis? He made his keyboardist look average in comparison. I couldn't help staring. His hair was the color of strong coffee, and he wore it long, the walnut waves hitting below his shoulders. His eyes shone a soft hazel green. His face boasted high cheekbones and a perfectly formed nose, and those lips... The most amazing lips I'd ever seen on a man—full and flawless. I'd gawked at photos of him in magazines, not believing it was possible for a man to be quite so perfect-looking—beautiful and rugged handsome at the same time.

Not that I could see any of this at the moment, with the blonde on top of him blocking most of my view.

I looked down at my phone once more. My driver was still fifteen minutes away. Crap.

Then I looked up.

Straight into the piercing eyes of Jett Draconis.

This story continues in
Misadventures with a Rock Star!

ACKNOWLEDGMENTS

Thank you to my husband, John, my biggest fan, my support system, my rock, and the reason I started writing in the first place. I love you.

I would also like to thank the entire team at Waterhouse Press, particularly David, Jon, Meredith, and Scott. You guys have been incredible and I am simply in awe at your level of talent. A huge thank you to all the readers out there, I feel incredibly blessed to share my stories.

MORE MISADVENTURES

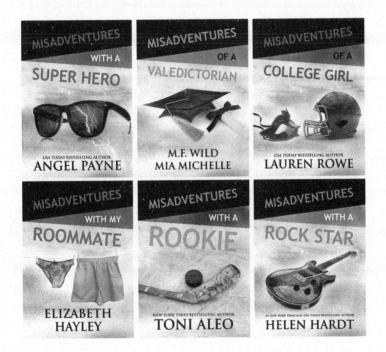

**VISIT MISADVENTURES.COM
FOR MORE INFORMATION!**

MORE MISADVENTURES

VISIT MISADVENTURES.COM
FOR MORE INFORMATION!